NEW MADRID

THE CERTAINTY OF UNCERTAINTY

MALCOLM BAILEY

Disclaimer: This story is fiction. Characters, situations, locations and names were created by the author's imagination. Resemblance to real events, persons, dead or alive is coincidental.

ISBN: 978-1-54394-989-6 (print)
ISBN: 978-1-54394-990-2 (ebook)

To the memory of John L .Bailey and Kenneth Brassell

CONTENTS

TOO MANY IRONS IN THE FIRE

"DEAN WOODMAN IS COMING!" TAMMIE DOAN SHOUTED down the hall, as the dean's high heels clicked determinedly towards the teacher's assistants guarding the classroom door.

"Where in the world is he?" Mary Morrow questioned from the doorway of Anthropology 402. "Try to stall Woodman, and I'll call John again on his cell phone. We should be able to reach him."

Two blocks away, John Conners' truck bucked and sputtered down Getwell Street in the heart of Memphis, Tennessee. He was on his way back to the University of Memphis.

Oh, no! Don't do this to me now, he thought.

John was in such a hurry to leave his Coahoma County, Mississippi, excavation site, seventy-five miles back, that he did not check the fuel supply before he left. The hand on his gauge sat below the 'E' now. Forward motion of the truck had not stopped yet only because it was headed downhill and had a little momentum left.

1

John Conners and his truck slowly and silently rolled forward. With great skill and luck, he coaxed the vehicle into the University of Memphis parking lot and into his designated spot.

Dean Woodman now stood at the classroom door of Anthropology 402, tapping her foot.

"Mary, where is John? He told me he would be here to instruct this class today. That man! Ugh!" Woodman shook her head.

"I know. I know, Dr. Woodman. I thought he would be here, too! I've started the class, and the students are watching a film that he wanted them to see today. They haven't missed anything yet," replied Mary.

"Keep the class then, but when you see that irresponsible, scatterbrained man, tell him to come straight to my office." The dean stormed off down the hall.

Dean Woodman ran a tight ship. She had always been considered highly intelligent, and hence, was well respected. She was the firstborn of a large family. When her mother passed away, she was expected to discipline and support her siblings. After rearing her two brothers and three sisters, Woodman decided against family life and devoted herself to academia. Once out of the house, she worked her way through college, and thereafter became the best department chair the university had ever had.

Mary again called John's cell phone. Getting no answer, she left a message. "John, this is Mary. The dean has been here. She wants to see you, pronto." Mary shut off her smartphone and went back to overseeing the class.

Out in the parking lot, John Conners gathered his latest treasure up from the covered bed of his twenty-year-old truck and packed the object neatly with straw into a midsized wooden crate. Gently, he set the crate on a dolly, and hurried—as carefully as he could—to get inside the building. Out of habit, he checked his cell phone for messages and calls, only to discover the battery was dead. Again.

As John neared the doorway to the darkened classroom, he could hear the voice of the film's narrator describing the migration of Native Americans from Asia to the interior of North America. John saw Mary, and he was relieved that she had been there to start his class. She had covered for him. What a girl!

"Hi, Mary! Thanks, you really saved me … again … uh… I can explain."

"Hi, John. It's OK, I know how you get distracted sometimes," Mary said, happy to see him. "I was really worried. The dean was here, and she was really steamed. Where have you been? I left a message for you on your phone."

"Sorry, my phone battery has been down. My charger is broken again. I stayed at the dig all night. Accidentally fell asleep. But look!" His face broke into a huge smile as his hand swept toward the treasure that he brought from the Coahoma dig. He pointed to the crate on the dolly. "We found a cypress dugout canoe that was caught in an old fish weir, the type I've been studying for some time now. The old river changed course and revealed the canoe that was buried under layers of sand and clay for hundreds of years. I hope to have it displayed in the Mississippi Museum of Natural History once it is fully studied. It is such a unique find."

"Yes, John, I remember that you wrote a book about fish weirs."

John nodded, pleased that she remembered his work. "Anyway, it gets better. There was a metal armor breastplate and a helmet from Hernando Desoto's time period on a complete skeleton. The canoe was shot full of arrows, and there was an arrowhead lodged in the skeleton's neck that was found wearing the armor."

John offered her a look inside the straw-filled crate.

"It's the best example of early pottery I've ever found. It's completely intact and is sealed with beeswax and tar. I just couldn't leave it half buried there, so last night I kept working to free it. Guess I fell asleep when I went back to my truck, and the next thing I knew, the sunrise woke me up. I finished unearthing it and rushed back here. My truck nearly ran out of gas on the way back and well. . . ."

Mary smiled. "That's a good story, John, but you'll have to tell Dean Woodman so she understands what happened. She was tapping her foot and obviously irritated at you."

"OK. How much longer is the movie?"

"It's almost over. I'll finish up the class for you so you can go see the dean."

"Thanks! Come by my office later?"

"Sure," Mary said, flashing her warm, beautiful smile, as she turned and walked away.

Mary Baker Morrow was twenty-six years old and very beautiful. Her quick smiles and positive attitude energized anyone near her, and she set the mood wherever she went. She was a green-eyed brunette with clear, healthy skin, short, clear-coated nails, and long, slender hands and feet.

Mary loved to help people, especially when it meant a meeting of the minds or elevating knowledge. A natural-born teacher, she had always been interested in history and archeology, and had the proof in the form of a kindergarten self-portrait she drew in a box of memorabilia. "When I grow up, I want to be an Archeologist" the study in crayon declared, alongside a figure of a girl wearing a boonie hat and holding a trowel.

Mary and John had been dating for two years. They liked each other from the moment they met. Archeology, music, and cooking were their shared delights. Mary loved to bake artisan breads, and John was a charcoal grill master.

Phone conversations between them frequently lasted from thirty minutes to an hour or longer. Like teenagers, the couple spent hours sharing their favorite stories from their childhoods and their most private dreams for the future. John had never felt this way about anyone else, nor had Mary.

John set the relic carefully on his office desk and then went directly to the dean's office.

"Hi, Dean Woodman," he said and promptly smiled and winked at her.

"Don't 'hi' me," she replied. "Where have you been? How do you expect me to take you seriously as a Ph.D. candidate and instructor when you don't do what you say you will do?"

"I know. It looks bad. I won't let it happen again, Dean. I just get so wound up in my work at the dig. You won't believe the relic that I just found! I fell asleep trying to get it all out of the ground before daybreak, and I didn't wake up early enough to get back here on time. My truck ran out of gas, and I … well … I … "

"OK, OK, I get the picture," Dean Woodman said, as she slammed the manila folder holding John's record of service down on the desk. "This has happened several times, and you always have an excuse. See that it doesn't happen again, or I'll have to terminate your position here. Do you understand?"

Her face contorted and her brow tightened. John knew that she meant business this time.

"Yes, Dean. Certainly! I really need this job and a chance to finish my Ph.D."

John almost bowed as he backed out of the door from Dean Woodman's office. He closed the door softly and wiped his brow with relief while catching his breath.

John hurried back to his office and studied the sealed terra-cotta jar. Sandy, clay dirt clung to the sides and lay caked around the rim. John spread out newspapers to catch the debris as he meticulously cleaned up the jar. He proceeded to photograph and measure the relic, making copious notes.

"Knock! Knock!" Mary said as she opened the outdated, frosted-glass office door. John's office was about twenty feet wide and thirty feet long. The ceiling was twelve feet high and lit by floor-to-ceiling windows and florescent light fixtures. Along the walls were makeshift wooden shelves stacked high with plastic bins full of skeleton fragments, potshards, arrowheads, and celts. These specimens were all carefully tagged and recorded. On the wall directly behind John's desk was a huge map of Arkansas, Mississippi, Missouri, and Tennessee. John had spent many hours marking archeological sites that he had worked on and sites that he hoped to work in the future. There was so much to do and so little time.

Mary peeked around the door. She saw John and smiled. "So that's it!"

"Come on in, Mary." John's voice was animated with excitement. "As soon as the outside is cleaned, we'll open this jar. I'm still wondering what this design is on the top."

"May I help, too?" Tammie Doan asked as she scurried behind Mary into the room. "I just dismissed my class, and I'm ready to discover!"

"Sure, have a seat."

With gloved hands, they all worked quickly and quietly, not saying a word, until John finally got the figure on the top of the jar clean.

"This is a bear emblem. I've seen it a few times before, but it's a lot older than the artifacts from the Desoto expedition."

Carefully, John bound the jar with soft fabric and tape in an attempt to prevent breakage. After carefully cutting a line through the wax with a knife, John turned to Tammie and said, "You and Mary hold on to this jar, while I pry the lid open."

John and the two women tugged and pulled until the lid finally gave way a little.

"I think it moved," John announced. "Steady . . . "

He pulled up on the lid and eased it back and forth, gently, until it was free. Nervously, he grabbed the powerful, yet small flashlight from his pocket. Realizing one wrong move could destroy the precious vessel, John reminded himself to stay calm. All three were so anxious to see the contents, as they each leaned over the opening, that their heads bumped together. Each obscured the view from the others, and no one could see inside the jar! They all three stepped back, laughing from embarrassment. Civility emerged, and John was given the first opportunity to view the interior of the clay vessel. What he saw could be withdrawn from the jar more easily if the mouth of the jar was near the table surface.

"Stand back. I'm going to turn it on its side."

As he moved the jar, the edge of a thin cypress board slid out. A thin sheet of metal, possibly hammered gold, covered the board.

There were more of these metal-covered boards and some cypress boards without metal that were treated with a type of wax substance, similar to the seal of the jar. The waxy coating on the boards was like modern-day polyurethane. With great care, a total of two dozen very thin boards, or plates, as John now referred to them, were liberated. Each one displayed symbols on every available surface.

"This is exciting! Do you think this is real gold?"

"Yes, I do," John said.

Mary's face had turned from its usual peaches and cream to a bright red glow. Her eyes sparkled as she looked at the treasure. "This is amazing!"

"Yes, I know!" John agreed.

"I love it, too!" Tammie chimed in. "How old do you think it is?"

"I think we may have something really old and special," John said. "Probably 500 B.C., at least for the things that we have found so far."

John tested the metal for identification. Several physical tests were performed on one of the plates, including a test for hardness. Mary picked up the flashlight and illuminated the inside of the jar.

"EEEEEHHHH!" She squealed with delight. "There's something else in the bottom, John. It looks like little toys! It's a bear, a man, and a woman, and then what looks like a different set of warrior people with weapons and shields. There is even a little campfire! Something else, John . . . I think they're all made of gold."

"That's fantastic! We never have found gold in any of the sites in the Mississippi River area. That explorer must have lost his life over this. These artifacts must have been very important to the people from whom they were taken," John surmised. "Get the long tongs out of the closet over behind my desk. I'll try to get them out without breaking the jar. Tammie, could you get my other camera in the top desk drawer? I need to take pictures of all this stuff. We need to keep good records of every centimeter of these artifacts."

Mary carefully laid out the plates and the small figures and began to take photographs. She indicated the date and included a ruler in the photo of the pieces so a reference of size would be shown in each picture.

"Look! Here is a book . . . a journal! The explorer must have sealed it inside the jar for safe keeping during his escape." It's in Spanish. John, I think I recognize the words. My Spanish is rusty, but I have a computer program on my laptop that can help us get the translation."

"Great! Go get it, and let's see what was so important to go to all the trouble to preserve the jar and the contents."

Mary was soon back and loading the foreign words into her program. The screen looked like a giant spreadsheet as she loaded letters into each block. The screen began to fill with possible inter-pretations. The three researchers sat like small children peering at a TV screen during their favorite cartoon. They were glued to it with fervent anticipation.

After half an hour, the results were ready to print.

"I think we have something," Mary said.

"Print away!" John gave her a thumbs-up gesture.

The newly printed pages rushed one after another onto the printer tray. Mary picked them up and double-checked their order. John and Tammie each found a chair, sat comfortably, and listened intently as Mary proceeded to read aloud the computer-generated translation of the journal.

This is my journal. My name is Captain Juan Carlos Ramirez. My men and I were scouting for our expedition company and came across a tribe of Indians that welcomed us to their camp. They had never seen white people before and treated us well. After a few pleasant days as guests at their camp, we were told the tribe's greatest legend. This is a record of the tale, and the wooden plates show a map of the sacred cave and altar where gold offerings were made.

An Indian brave named Manapah, of a place on the east side of the great water, where the sun rises, left his tribe to find meat to provide food for his people. There had been a devastating outbreak of sickness that killed all the wildlife in his traditional hunting grounds.

"The South had periodic outbreaks of anthrax during droughts." John interrupted to explain.

Manapah was in his mid-twenties, was over six feet tall, very strong and wiry. He had large, muscular arms and supple hands. He was the chief's favorite son and had many friends throughout his tribe. The drought had devastated his tribe, and he wanted to do what he could to save them.

He crossed the great river to the west bank in a dug-out cypress canoe. After days of tracking, he stalked and killed a huge buck. This brought him great happiness. Now, he could save his people from starvation with freshly cured meat of the deer. He would take the meat back and convince his tribe to send a large hunting party to this area and get enough food for all his people to last throughout the winter.

Manapah prepared the meat for drying over an open fire. He started constructing a drag made of small sapling oak trees. He would load all the cured meat in a sling between the trunks and in such a way be able to transport a heavy load easily. Then, without warning, the woods became silent. Suddenly, he was knocked unconscious by an arrow with a large, blunt tip, striking him on the right temple just above and behind his ear. When Manapah awoke, he was tied to a tree. An angry mob of men from the Quan Pawtee tribe was sitting around a large campfire close by. One of them got up and confronted Manapah.

He said, "You dishonor our chief by killing the great dominant buck. Only our chief is allowed to kill this deer. He has chosen not to kill this animal. This buck was to roam the forests and sire many large bucks. For this, you must die." The man who said this was Ohototo, the Quan Pawtee chief's son.

"I did not know," Manapah said.

The men around the fire began to taunt Manapah. They picked up clods of dirt and hurled them at him. Some pieces hit Manapah in the face. The brave struggled to get free, but it was no use. He was bound too tightly. Some of the men laughed and proceeded to throw knives at Manapah. It was obvious that the intent was to frighten, but not kill, Manapah at this time, although some blades came very close to his flesh. Then the men got out their bows and began to shoot arrows at him. Again, they displayed their skills by accurately missing Manapah. Ohototo got up from his mat on the ground and said, "Let him suffer now in the hot sun with no water or food. We will bring him before the tribal council tomorrow and decide how he will die."

The day wore on and Manapah suffered there. His arms and legs cramped and hurt from being unable to sit or lay down. Once he noticed a beautiful young woman carrying a pot of water. He longed for a drink. As she poured the water around some squash plants, she glanced in his direction and smiled. Manapah could not believe it. He smiled back, and the beautiful girl blushed and looked away. Later that day, the men of the tribe had gone out hunting and no one was paying attention to Manapah. The young girl walked up to the tree with a cup of water and carefully gave Manapah a drink. He was overjoyed. She looked into his eyes for a moment.

From a short distance away, a strong male voice shouted at the girl, "Minatomeh, what are you doing? Get away from him!" The girl jumped back, startled. The man was her father coming out of his hut.

"Father, may I speak?" Minatomeh, the chief's daughter, asked. "Do you remember the dream that I had last month?"

"Yes, the one which our shaman said was a vision from the spirit world. Why does it matter now, Minatomeh?"

"This man . . . he must be the one that I was prophesied to marry. He is a stranger like the one in my dream, and I am to marry him and have many strong children."

She begged the chief not to kill Manapah.

After much arguing with Minatomeh, the chief agreed to allow Manapah to live, but the chief continued to question the young brave's ability to be deserving of his daughter. The greatest test the chief could reasonably imagine for their captive would be to fight and dominate the Great Spirit bear.

The chief declared, "He must bring back proof of the battle. A claw from one of the bear's front paws. It must show the white band that no other bear possesses. It is a difficult task and has never been done except by the elder one, the Great Father of our tribe, who has gone on before us. The Great Spirit bears all have unusual claws that are banded as no other bears. The young warrior must bring back a claw but not harm the bear in any other way."

When presented with this challenge, Manapah agreed to go through the trial.

The chief said, "He is spared for now. He may marry my daughter and live as one of us if he succeeds, but if he fails, he will be killed."

The chief's daughter was five feet and eight inches tall, slim, and had beautiful long black hair down to her small waist. Her skin was clear and bronze. She had large, almond-shaped eyes. Her smile was enchanting and showed perfect teeth. Minatomeh moved gracefully everywhere she went and was, without question, a true beauty.

Manapah was freed. He was allowed three days to recuperate and then went to the woods to hunt the bear.

As a brave, Manapah was at home in the wilderness and could find food and water. He continued to heal, even as he searched for the bear.

On the second day, he found signs of a bear and followed them into a massive cave. For days and days, he tracked the bear through the cave. Manapah lost track of the number of days as he moved through the darkness of a cave with only the light of one torch burning at a time. The trail finally came out of the cave, very far to the north, but Manapah had not seen or heard the bear. So, he continued to search for tracks.

Later that day, tired and hungry, Manapah found faint bear tracks, and was on its trail again. This time, they were very faint, partly erased by a recent rain. Then, suddenly, to his amazement, there was, before him, a huge ball of black fur, in a massive net bag hanging from ropes, tied to two trees. The entire animal had been hoisted about four feet above the ground in a trap made by man.

Carefully, Manapah drew closer to the animal. It was the great bear he had been tracking. The bear's neck was entangled with rope. He appeared lifeless. Slowly and cautiously, Manapah withdrew his knife from his scabbard and surveyed the animal, trying to find a paw and more importantly, the white-ringed claw.

As he reached through the net and gently selected a toe, something caught Manapah's eye. Was this bear alive? *No,* he thought. *He is dead.* But then Manapah caught a movement. What moved? Then he noticed the bear's eyelid twitch—just once. Was he seeing things? On second glance, the eyelid twitched again. He quickly decided he would take the claw and then he would cut the great bear free rather than dishonor the great spirit of the animal by killing it, or allowing it to be killed. Manapah would willingly risk his own life by freeing an angry bear. After all, according to the challenge, the bear was not to be harmed.

Manapah knew he was now in woods that were claimed by the fierce Irraquaro people. He had heard many stories about these people. They were known to surround neighboring tribes at night and attack without mercy. They killed the men and carried off the women and children and forced them to become members of their tribe.

This trap must be one of theirs, he thought. *The hunters have not come by to check their trap yet. They will be back soon. I must hurry and harvest the claw.* With great care, he cut the claw away from the quick. He knew the cut would not be painful, and that the claw would grow back without damage. The great bear jerked his paw back as the claw came loose. Manapah carefully wrapped the claw in cloth and tied the small package securely to his upper thigh, under his clothing.

Then Manapah cut the ropes, and the great bear tumbled to the ground. With knife in hand, Manapah looked on as the bear snorted and kicked free of the remaining net. The bear did not turn in anger to Manapah, but ran free, with gratitude, down the trail. At that moment, the Irraquaro hunters appeared from the other side of the trail. It took only a quick look for them to see what had happened. Furious yelps and war cries went up from the warriors when they realized that Manapah had freed their prize catch.

After a brief chase and struggle between Manapah and ten Irraquaro warriors, Manapah was captured and taken back to camp to be sacrificed. The tribe was in a frenzy. Meat was cooked. Special vegetables and herbs were prepared. The members of the tribe smoked from a communal pipe so all the people would experience the spirit of the celebration.

Ritual dancing to the beat of many pounding drums began around the camp. All was aglow around the bonfire blazing in the camp's center. The men started for Manapah. They were chanting, turning, brandishing stone hatchets and spears at imaginary enemies and game. The warriors then picked Manapah up and placed him on a large, flat, stone altar. He was to be torn apart, as enacted by the warriors' gestures. The chief raised a sharp, stone knife and looked into Manapah's frightened eyes and then up, into the heavens.

Suddenly, blood-curdling screams from the tribesmen were heard, across the ceremonial grounds, and chaos ensued as the Great Spirit bear appeared, slashing his way through the camp gathering. So startled were the Irraquaro that they released their grip on Manapah. In no time, he had escaped into the deep woods, back toward the cave. No Irraquaro noticed Manapah's escape because they were fleeing the attack of the massive, enraged bear. The bear dropped from his full upright stance of fourteen feet and gave chase to all who were there.

Manapah kept running as fast as his feet would carry him after he reached the cave passages. As the Irraquaro frequently went into this cave for religious celebrations, they left many torches at the entrance of the cave. Manapah quickly grabbed a burning torch and threw the rest down a deep ravine. He was able to keep the torch going as he moved with great speed.

The Great Spirit bear slayed many of the tribe before he finally tired and turned away. The tribe was in disarray and exhausted. When they regrouped after the bear had disappeared into the deep forest, they soon realized that Manapah had escaped. A few warriors remembered seeing Manapah disappearing on the path to the cave, and the warriors decided to give chase to the outsider that had dishonored their tribe by releasing their catch.

At daybreak, the Irraquaro followed his trail into the cave. They did not know that they, too, were being followed.

The chase went on for days throughout the massive cave. Knowing that the combustible material for his torch would soon be depleted, Manapah searched and found deadwood and abandoned nests that had been washed into the caves many years ago. He spent nearly half a day trying to find the right materials to replenish his torch, a costly use of time, as he realized the Irraquaro would now be close behind him.

He was almost back to the Quan Pawtee main camp, but still in the cave, when the Irraquaro caught up with him. An arrow that glanced off the side of the rock-lined cave wall wounded him in the leg. Manapah was at a higher elevation than his enemies, but not in a position to avoid them. He managed to shove rocks down on several pursuers, but the rocks had little effect. An escape looked hopeless until the bear appeared again behind the Irraquaro in the narrowest part of the cave. The bear slashed and mauled six of the twelve warriors. It looked as if the men might get away through a passage that was so narrow that the bear could not pursue them.

Then it happened. There was a great rumble in the floor of the cave. The walls shook. Rocks fell from the roof. It was a great earthquake. In seconds, three of the warriors were swallowed up into a chasm in the floor of the cave. The remaining three Irraquaro tribesmen turned and ran for home, screaming that the Great Spirit bear had caused the earthquake and that the spirit was too strong. They vowed they would never return.

The earthquake had created a huge divide that separated the warriors and Spirit bear on one side of the cave and Manapah on the other side. The great bear let out a loud growl and turned and went back the way that he had come. The deep fissure caused by the earthquake and the presence of the Spirit Bear forever after kept the Quan Pawtee people safe.

Manapah gave a sigh of relief. He turned and followed the path out of the cave and back, at last, to the Quan Pawtee tribe and their beautiful princess. All in the tribe were elated and surprised to see him. Manapah proudly presented the special claw to the chief.

A great celebration was given for him, and his wedding to the princess followed. They sent meat to Manapah's tribe and lived in peace ever after. The Quan Pawtee people looked to the bear as their protector spirit from that time and delivered gifts to the Great Spirit bear every year. They traveled down the great running water to the

17

coast and traded with the people of the Western Gulf for gold and silver and fashioned metal animals to thank the spirit bear for protecting them.

Many years passed, and floods and other earthquakes finally closed the entrance to the cave, but the people kept the stories of the past alive by oral tradition. Each generation passed the legend of Manapah down by listening to the chief tell the story around the campfire. After many, many generations passed, the people began to think the stories were only fanciful legends.

Mary scanned the rest of the document. "The journal says that the explorers found the cave by accident and took one of the many golden bear statues. His two fellow explorers developed fever and died before they could escape. The surviving explorer says that the treasure was too large for him to carry alone. He decided he would get back to the expedition. His plan was to return with more men and horses to retrieve the remaining treasure."

When the journal came to an end, Mary stopped speaking.

"He never made any other entries. He must have sealed this part of the treasure and the journal in the jar for safe keeping. The explorer probably was discovered and chased down when the people found out he had tried to slip away with treasure. They must have known that several arrows had hit him, but he was able to get far enough away that the tribe never found him. He must have been caught in that old, abandoned fish weir and died. The flood waters of the Mississippi covered his body with mud until the site was excavated." John pieced together the probability of the journal's author.

"The big treasure could still be there!" Mary said.

"Maybe, just maybe!" John replied. "I think I'll get in touch with my old friend, Mark McKenzie, and his wife, Marissa. They always like a good mystery."

MARK AND MARISSA

MARK AND MARISSA MCKENZIE WERE YOUNG, MOTI-
vated, and well educated.

Mark worked in the financial world, placing institutional invest-
ments, and Marissa was an OB/GYN resident at the University of
Tennessee in Memphis. She was in her last year of the program, and
was very obviously seven months pregnant.

Mark spent a great deal of time visiting clients and advising them
about proper investment strategy. When not at work, he played golf,
spent time cooking gourmet meals with Marissa, and enjoyed ama-
teur archeology, digging and caving with his archeologist friend,
John Conners.

Mark and John had mapped many caves in Mexico and the western United States.

Mark kissed his wife gingerly. "I'm off to work. Won't be back
until late tonight on an American Airlines flight. Then, John Conners
has a dig site in Coahoma County close to Clarksdale, down in the

Mississippi Delta, that he wants to show me. I'll drive down there early in the morning. Since you have a forty-eight-hour shift, you'll not be home, anyway."

He smiled, stepped even closer, and gave her a good-bye embrace, pulling away to gently caress her baby bump. Marissa was about to pop, so to speak. She was taking advantage of every minute she could to stay in bed before preparing to go to the hospital for early rounds.

"It won't be much longer until you finish. This is your last year of residency. It's going by quickly, now," Mark said.

"Yes, I know you're right. Have a safe trip. I can't wait until you get back," replied Marissa.

Mark added apologetically, "Sorry I had to get up so early, but the flight is at 7:00 and I have some spreadsheets to review before I talk to the clients."

"It's OK."

"Be sure to set the alarm after I'm gone."

A moment later she heard the garage door open and shut. He was on his way. She rolled out of bed and set the house alarm again.

This was one of the loneliest times for Marissa in the week. She would not see Mark for another two days. She looked at her bedside clock and saw that she had half an hour naptime left before the 5 a.m. alarm. She would have plenty of time to shower and be at the medical center by six o'clock.

One course of study in her fourth year of residency was described in the medical school catalogue as Gynecological Oncology. The time required was stated to be twelve hours a day. Everyone knew it really required sixteen-hour days, and in many cases, the resident was frequently expected to pull twenty-four or forty-eight hour shifts. She was seven months, plus a few days, pregnant. Every minute of sleep was precious.

She crawled back under the covers, fluffed up her pillow, assumed her traditional right-sided fetal position, and immediately fell asleep.

Ring! Ring! Ring! The ear-piercing sounds of a demanding smartphone shattered the perfect silence. Marissa shot up in bed and awkwardly managed to move across it to pick up the smartphone on the nightstand.

"Hello? Hello!" There was dead silence.

"Mark, is that you? Are you alright?"

Silence. The line was still open, but there was no identification on caller ID. Then a click, and the phone returned to the home screen.

Marissa's heart was pounding. Very few people knew her smartphone number.

She quickly dialed Mark.

"Mark, did you just call?"

"No, hun. Why?"

"I just got a call, and no one said anything."

"Look on the caller ID. What's it say?"

"I already did. It just says 'unknown number.'"

"It was probably just a random, misdialed call or a robo call. They were probably too embarrassed to say anything."

"I thought something happened to you. It scared me," Marissa said.

"No, everything's all right. If it keeps happening, you can call your dad if I'm already in the air."

"OK, it's probably nothing. I love you. Bye."

"Love you, too. Bye, hun."

No sooner than Mark had said goodbye Marissa felt a wave of pain grip her torso. It was a deep, gripping sensation that enveloped her lower body as if all her muscles were cramping at once. She went to her knees as the waves of pain rushed through her. Was she having the baby now? Was something wrong? It was all she could do to get to the phone again and dial Mark. After two rings, he answered.

"Mark!" she gasped. "Something's wrong. I'm hurting."

"Is it the baby?"

"I don't know. I'm about to pass out!"

"Hold on . . . I'll be right there! Hold on, hun. Keep talking to me!"

At that point Marissa began to gasp and cry.

"I'm on my way! Hold on, hold on!" Mark said as he made a quick turn and headed back to their home.

"Uh, oh!" Marissa said under her breath. She leaned forward and curled up to ease the pain.

She was relieved when Mark rushed into the bedroom soon after. He picked her up and whisked her away to the emergency room.

Half an hour later, the chief resident came into the hospital room. "You're fine, Marissa. False labor," she said. "I know how you feel. I had the same thing happen to me last year. Felt terrible, but now I have a healthy one-year-old. Don't worry. This may happen several times." She smiled and turned to face Mark. "We'll keep her here for forty-eight hours to observe. Go on and catch your plane. She'll be fine."

"I-I should have known," Marissa said. "But it's different when it's you having the pains.

I'm sorry I got so upset and called you back, Mark. Thanks for rescuing me. I hope you can still catch your flight. I'll be here at the hospital anyway. I'll be alright."

"If you say so, Marissa. I love you." Mark smiled as he bent down and gave her a gentle kiss on her lips. "If you're sure?"

"I'm sure. I'm sorry. Please go!"

"OK, then."

"Bye. Tell John to bring Mary to see us. We'll have dinner?"

"OK, I'll call if they can."

Mark thanked everyone at the nurses' station as he left. It had been an exciting morning.

A FALL TO REMEMBER

BEAR DADDY STOOD ON HIS FAVORITE ROCK. THIS ROCK was a huge flat outcropping of limestone on the side of the mountain, and it extended twenty feet over the valley. He smiled as he watched a bald eagle circling above the winding river, below, in that same valley. The afternoon sun gave a golden glow to the yellow and red fall leaves that clung to the branches of every tree in the area. They seemed especially beautiful this fall.

Every time Bear Daddy visited, it made him feel good, and it was not easy to feel good nowadays. Bear Daddy was the chief of the Quan Pawtees. His real name was Running Bear, but everyone liked the name Bear Daddy better. His family was descended from the great hunter, Manapah, and the princess, Minatomeh.

The Quan Pawtee people were now only a shadow of the tribe that was here before the European settlers arrived over four hundred years ago. Their territory had extended from what is now south-ern, central Missouri to the east, past the great river, known now as the Mississippi, and many miles south of that line. Bear Daddy's great-grandfather told him of the invaders that brought sickness and death in their blankets. Most of the tribe had been destroyed by disease and despair. Bear Daddy's family was almost wiped out later, when the Mississippi River flooded the valleys and ate up the farming and hunting lands.

Bear Daddy had survived several floods and had grown up strong and smart. He became the chief and leader of his people during a time of great cultural change and social awareness. It had been a difficult challenge for Bear Daddy, but he had guided his people well.

"Full Feather!" Bear Daddy's booming voice rang out and echoed off the barren rocky cliff across the valley and came back to him. "Full Feather, where are you? Where are you?"

Bear Daddy's eleven-year-old grandson was having a great time exploring the woods with his grandfather. Bear Daddy liked to take time to enjoy the woods and trails with the boy. One day, Full Feather would be the chief and Bear Daddy wanted him to develop an appreciation for nature and this land.

There was no answer, and daylight was waning. Bear Daddy started down the trail that Full Feather had taken earlier.

The wind was still hot. Every now and then, a dust cloud spun aimlessly back and forth across the trail in front of him. Bear Daddy's grandfather used to say that the dust devils were unhappy spirits of lost souls who had not been allowed to pass into the next world. The dust devils were forced to wander the world until a person with a pure soul took pity on them. This person would have to catch the dust devil in a deerskin bag and then burn the bag over a roaring hot, pinecone fire and throw the cooled ashes to the four winds from a southern-facing cliff. The spirit would then be free.

He saw the ceremony done many times and felt elation to know that a person's spirit had been released.

Farther down the trail, Full Feather sat and watched a brown squirrel with one floppy ear. The animal stood up on his hind legs and balanced by curling his fluffy tail into an "s" shape. As if in deep thought, the squirrel looked left, and then right, and popped two huge acorns into each cheek for easy transport. He knew that these acorns must be stored in the most secure place that he could put them. The squirrel scurried along the ground to a place he had discovered earlier.

Full Feather climbed up a nearby weeping willow tree so he could continue to watch the squirrel as the furry creature raced across the forest floor. He watched the funny, flop-eared squirrel duck into some thick brush near a freshly fallen rockslide. The inquisitive boy jumped out of the tree and ran toward the place where the squirrel had just vanished. To his surprise, the hiding place for the squirrel was bigger than a hollow log or a space under a rock. There before him was the opening to a cave! Fresh dirt made it look as though it had just been turned over, as in a cornfield, around the opening. Tumbled rocks lay everywhere without a pattern. There was just enough sunlight getting into the cave opening to light up the entrance and a short way toward the inside.

"Full Feather, come here. Where are you?" Bear Daddy implored.

Still no answer came back. Bear Daddy always had trouble with Full Feather's curious nature.

Then, from the trail ahead, near the rock cliff, Full Feather yelled, "I'll be back soon. There's a cave here. It's huge!"

Bear Daddy heard him faintly.

"If you don't come back here right now, you won't get any honey on your flat cakes tonight. No blueberries either!"

Bear Daddy was frustrated with the youth's strong will, but deep down inside, he was proud of the child's fiercely independent nature.

"Grandfather, look!" Full Feather shouted. "It's a big opening in the mountain. Come see! I'm in a big, big cave. Over here!"

Full Feather, again, followed the squirrel's path toward the place where he had been storing his acorns in the cave. A large pile of rubble lined the opening of the cave. Upon entering the mouth of the cave, Full Feather was amazed when he discovered a huge crack running northwest to southeast, along the side of the cave wall. It appeared to go on and on, but the late afternoon light was too dim to determine how large the cave or the crack really was.

Bear Daddy finally caught up with Full Feather. Full Feather saw the squirrel on the edge of the crack. "I'm going to catch him, Bear Daddy!"

"No! No, don't!" Bear Daddy cautioned.

At that same moment, the rock crunched and crumbled beneath Full Feather's foot, throwing him off balance. The boy began to fall toward the cold, black void of the crevice.

"Ahhhhh-eeeeh!" he screamed. Bear Daddy lunged and reached for him. Time seemed to slow. Bear Daddy could feel his arm stretch.

"Ahhh-eeeh!" he heard again. The tiny fingers twisted in the air in front of him. He saw pieces of dirt flying in the air alongside tiny rocks; they seemed to freeze in midair. Bear Daddy caught a glimpse of Full Feather's eyes, then broke away to focus on his outstretched hand.

"Full Featherrrrr! Oh, Great Spirit, help us!"

The sounds bounced off the cave walls, the same sound that had been made throughout the ages; man's plea to his God for help in times of great need when all else fails.

Then their hands met. Of all the times Bear Daddy had caught and held on to anything throughout his life, the most precious grasp had come to this. He had to hold on to Full Feather. He had to!

"Oh, no!"

Full Feather's hand slipped through Bear Daddy's fingers.

In an instant, the unthinkable had happened. A seemingly random set of events came together to magnify the lack of control human beings have over their lives.

But then, the heavy stainless-steel hook on Full Feather's backpack caught Bear Daddy's thick, nylon watchstrap and held long enough for Bear Daddy to reach once again and regain his grasp on Full Feather's hand. The fall was stopped. They both took a deep breath.

"Hold on!" Bear Daddy shouted.

"Hold on!"

Bear Daddy braced his legs and pushed with his left hand against the cave floor.

"Ugh. Pull up, Full Feather. Now!" They both strained, and at last, Full Feather crawled over the craggy rock edge. "Are you alright, Full Feather?"

"Yes, yes. How about you, Grandfather?"

"Yes, I'm OK."

"I thought you were gone."

Bear Daddy took a deep breath again and sighed. He gave Full Feather a hug. Bear Daddy then placed both hands on his grandson's shoulders, and set the boy away, the distance of his outstretched, aging, arms. Looking straight into the boy's eyes, the grandfather sternly said, "You must not act before you think about what could happen next. You are to become a leader of our people. Your decisions are not yours alone."

"Yes, I understand." Full Feather lowered his head. "I not only endangered myself but you also. I, I understand. I'm-I'm-I'm sorry. It won't happen again."

Bear Daddy nodded his head to show silent acceptance and closure.

"A lesson is clear to me," said Bear Daddy. "Do not lose faith in your creator, no matter how hopeless things may appear. The watch and backpack are both modern inventions and culturally alien to us, but they both helped us survive, so all things new are not wholly bad."

The two turned to walk back. Full Feather pointed. "Look over there!"

"Where?" Bear Daddy asked.

"There!"

He pointed to the corner of the wall near the back of the cave. It looked like polished stone, and next to it were several fairly crude, but still easily recognizable, drawings of different animals and people running. The picture of a large bear was prominent. It was too dark to see much more.

"This reminds me of the stories my grandfather told us around the tribal fire," Bear Daddy said. "This is amazing. I don't think that I have ever heard of any cave painting that has been discovered in this area, although some have been found in caves due west of here. We'll have to tell our friend, John Conners. He will know what to do with this place. He is the best archeologist in this area."

"What's an archeologist?" asked Full Feather.

"A person that studies the past by looking at old places where people have lived and worked. The archeologist carefully, step by step, records all the information that is available from these physical sites. For now, we need to get home. I know how you like to explore, but it's late and your grandmother will worry if we're not back soon. She will have supper ready and will be unhappy if we don't honor her by coming home on time."

Bear Daddy nodded his head as if agreeing with himself.

"Yes, you are right." Full Feather smiled at his grandfather and nodded his head also. They went arm and arm up the trail. It was an adventure worthy of a great campfire story.

The two walked back to Bear Daddy's truck. It was a perfectly restored 1952 Chevrolet pickup. Bear Daddy was especially proud of it. He had done all the work himself.

"Let me drive, Grandfather. I can do it! I know how! I've watched you forever.

It's late and you know how much trouble you have seeing when you cross the old bridge that faces the setting sun. Remember? Please, Please!"

"Oh, alright, Full Feather. Just this once. Don't say a word about this to your grandmother. She would have a fit. We probably wouldn't get supper. You've got to help me to remember to call John Conners at the university and get him to come and look at our cave as soon as possible. Let this be our secret for now. We don't want anyone to harm our cave."

"OK, I will remind you to call as soon as we get back. Can I blow the horn?"

"Yes, but not too much. It will scare the animals."

The old trail had been widened into a single-lane dirt and gravel road. Tall pines and oaks lined the sides of the path. Descendants of ash trees that his ancestors used for construction of bows and arrows stood proud and healthy, full of leaves, in glorious, autumn colors. Full Feather grinned, as he held both hands tightly to the large steering wheel. He loved to be with his grandfather.

Up ahead, the road turned sharply to the west and led to a bridge that crossed a dried, and very deep riverbed. The wooden structure was built sixty years ago and should have been replaced by now, but due to a lack of funds and low usage, the bridge had been all but forgotten. When the bridge was built, it was only meant to carry very light trucks. It was made of creosote-treated poles and planks. Over the years, it had been repaired, but only just enough.

"Full Feather, I can't see. Can you see?" The sun glared in Bear Daddy's eyes.

"Yes, Grandfather, I see the bridge."

The road to the bridge dropped straight down, as it went from the top of the ridge, on which the two travelers were riding, to the narrow, but deep, crevasse that it crossed.

"Slow down! You've got to hit the bridge runners just right!" shouted the old man.

The sun was low in the sky now and beaming straight down the center of the bridge. Full Feather squinted and pulled down the sun visor. He really couldn't see at all. Then he applied the brakes to slow the truck.

As he turned to set up the approach to the bridge, Full Feather gasped.

"The brakes! The brakes aren't working!"

"They were fine on the way up here!" Bear Daddy said in disbelief. "I checked them myself."

Quickly Full Feather stuck his head out of the door window on the driver's side, to see better where the edge of the bridge met the road. He was too far to the left! He turned hard to the right on the metal steering wheel. The sack of beans, on which Full Feather was sitting to allow him to see over the dashboard, gave way under the pressure of the sudden movement and tore. Beans spilled everywhere.

"Hold on, Grandfather!"

Full Feather looked out of the window again. He could see the deep crevasse below. He realized that he had not been able to correct enough and was about to careen off this old wooden passage. His heart jumped to his throat as he felt the front left tire lose contact with the bridge. It spun aimlessly over the void. The tire had no direction, no foundation, and no result when it was turned.

Full Feather tried the brakes again.

"Pull to the right, Grandfather!" At that moment, the right wheel slipped off the runner and dropped onto the floor of the bridge with a thump.

"Full Feather, hold on!" Bear Daddy reached with his left hand and pulled the old steering wheel to the right, but the truck dipped down on the left side and did not pop back onto the wooden runners as anticipated. The tires squealed, as if complaining at being asked to do the impossible. Bear Daddy's toolbox slid across the metal and plank floor of the truck bed, rattling and toppling over, sending hammers and wrenches thundering against the thick metal of the truck bed's side.

"Pull the wheel sharply to the right and let go a little as soon as you feel it pop up," yelled Bear Daddy.

Just then, Bear Daddy lunged to the right side of the truck seat, opening the door in one fluid motion, and extended his outstretched body thru the open window frame, keeping his feet firmly set together on the truck floorboard.

"Ah! Grandfather!" Full Feather screamed.

Then, as if lifted by an invisible cable, the truck righted itself as the effect of the old man shifting his weight leveled out the truck. The wheels jumped back on the tracks, and the truck shot over the bridge like a luge crossing the finish line at the Winter Olympics.

"Downshift, Full Feather! It will slow us down. Pull the emergency brake!" Bear Daddy shouted as he struggled to regain his seat in the speeding truck. Dust flew everywhere.

Full Feather downshifted and pulled the emergency brake. The truck lurched. As it slowed, Full Feather was able to guide the truck down the road. At last, it slid to a careening stop. All was suddenly quiet.

"Wow! That was a close one," Bear Daddy exclaimed.

"We were great, Grandfather! What happened to the brakes?"

"I don't know. They worked just fine this morning," Bear Daddy said.

"When we started down the hill, I pushed the brake pedal over and over, but nothing happened. It just felt limp," replied Full Feather.

Bear Daddy got out of the truck and opened the hood. He checked the brake fluid reservoir and found it almost empty.

"That's strange. I just changed all the fluids last week. The brake fluid was perfectly fine when I checked it this morning."

Bear Daddy walked around to the side of the front right tire, dropped to the ground, and slid under the truck on his back. It was dusty and hard to see, so he ran his fingers along the brake line.

"Ouch!"

"You OK, Bear Daddy?"

"Yeah! Just nicked my finger on a metal splinter."

He carefully felt again and could tell by the way the brake line felt that a hacksaw blade had cut in the line. *Somebody did this on purpose,* he thought to himself. Somebody was trying to scare him, or worse yet, to get rid of him.

"Brake fluid got out through this crack in the line." He didn't want to scare Full Feather, so he hid the whole truth of how that crack appeared. "We are lucky that we weren't killed. You did some great driving back there, Full Feather. I'm glad that I had you along. Let's walk the rest of the way back. We'll call your grandmother from the diner at the crossroads. She will love to hear about our day."

The two weary adventurers locked the truck and walked down the rocky road. They discussed the exciting day and exaggerated their parts in it each time the story was told. This was destined to become a family treasure, maybe a tribal legend!

Bear Daddy found the old payphone in the diner in working order and called his wife.

"Marty, we had trouble with the truck. We need you to pick us up at the crossroads diner. Thanks, hun."

Bear Daddy and Full Feather sat on the bench under the diner's front porch for less than ten minutes before Marty drove up.

"Grandmother, I sure am glad you were able to pick us up so soon. What's for supper?"

"Your favorite. Chicken and dumplings. We're having flat cakes for dessert."

"Great!"

"Now, what have you two been up to?" Marty asked.

The stories were retold, but with a few details left out and some embellished. Marty was accustomed to tall tales from both of them, so she was not surprised.

"You must be careful, dear," she said. "I really think you need to have a real mechanic look at the truck before you two ride again."

"OK. Sure. I do, too. I'll tell you more about it later." Bear Daddy said along with a wink at Marty.

Bear Daddy awoke the next day and called his cousin, Tommy Lightfoot, to give him a ride and help him fix his truck. Lightfoot was a very good mechanic, and he quickly repaired the broken line. Bear Daddy drove home.

Bear Daddy was excited about the cave and decided to call John Conners, the archeologist, to tell him about the new discovery. He pulled out his pocket calendar and turned to the area where he kept the phone numbers that he called frequently to find John's number.

His mind began to race back over the events of the day before as he dialed and listened to the phone ring. "Mississippi Archeological Department. Rusty speaking."

"Hello, this is chief Running Bear. I would like to speak with John Conners."

"John, John!" he shouted. "It's for you. He says his name is Running Bear."

"Yeah, tell him I'll be right there. He's the chief of the Quan Pawtee tribe. Great guy."

John Conners graduated four years earlier from the University of Mississippi with a master's degree in Anthropology. He worked with the state archeological service for several years and liked it so much that he decided to get a Ph.D. in Anthropology. When he was accepted in the program at the University of Memphis, he was able to arrange his schedule so he could still keep a part-time spot with the state of Mississippi while he pursued his degree. John frequently did field work with college students from the surrounding area, including Ole Miss, Mississippi State, Delta State, and the University of Memphis. John's current group on this project had grown to six eager students. He referred to them, privately, as his gophers.

John was especially fond of Bear Daddy. Many times the old chief had let John come onto the reservation to do research about the area.

"Hello, Conners here."

"Yes, John. I hope I did not trouble you."

"No, Bear Daddy, not at all. I'm always glad to hear from you. What can I do for you?"

"Well, my grandson and I stumbled onto a cave on the reservation that we've never seen before. There are pictures and symbols drawn on the walls. It looks really old and undisturbed. I don't think anyone has been in this cave for a very long time. The opening seems to have been exposed by a rockslide. We had a large tremor last week. Earthquake area, you know. I want you to take a look at it. I think it is the cave that our legends describe."

"Sure, Bear Daddy! Wow! This sounds really good! Thanks for calling. I'll meet you at the usual place at the reservation gate tomorrow morning around six o'clock."

"Good, John, I'll see you there."

John hung up and turned to his team that was excavating the site.

"Listen up, guys," John smiled. "I've got a new site to check out. Rusty can take over for me here while I'm away. Y'all can go ahead and shut down for today. Everybody, have a great weekend!"

A cheer went up from the dusty, sweaty group. They were hot and tired, and this good news was welcomed by all to hear.

"I'll see y'all next week. And if this is as good as I think it may be, we'll close this site temporarily and work the new site. See you later."

John immediately thought of his friends Mark and Marissa McKenzie. Mark was an avid spelunker, and Marissa was fabulous at sorting out details and solving mysteries.

Mark had already planned to meet him tomorrow at the Coahoma site. So all John had to do now was change their meeting place to Missouri.

The call to Mark was made. After a few simple directions, Mark told John he would meet him at the Missouri reservation the next morning.

John gave the group at the Coahoma site a farewell wave and jumped into his old Chevy 4X4. When he turned the ignition key, he couldn't help but wonder if the old vehicle would respond. This was the second rebuilt engine he had put into this truck. The salary he earned from his part-time school job and the state archeological service was small, and to get by, he continued to patch up his high mileage truck. He had thought of quitting, but he loved his work and needed the income to continue to pursue his doctoral degree. He was one of the few special people in modern society who put the thrill of discovery and love of knowledge above money and comfort. To his delight, the engine fired up and he was off.

In the back of his truck were his excavation tools, a tarpaulin, cot, battery supply, an ice chest, and two ten-gallon water tanks. He always remembered to load up with water for hand washing and to cool the engine in case the truck overheated. He never forgot to pack his faithful ice chest with sandwich fixings and cold drinking water, so he would not have to waste time or money eating out when he was away from home. The sleeping cot was always kept in the back of the Blazer. There was no sense wasting money on a motel room. He was on a tight budget and trying to save a little money for when he married. Once on the road, he'd stop at the first truck stop he came across.

The truck stop in Helena, Arkansas, was busy. John filled up with gas. Every time he filled up, he thought about how much better it would be if we used natural gas or electricity to fuel our vehicles. John decided to get a cup of coffee to keep him awake for the long nighttime drive through the Arkansas farmland roads, then on into the hills of Missouri.

Oh, no! he thought. *Macbeth.*

He had been so excited about the cave that he totally had forgotten about his date to see Shakespeare's play with Mary. John pulled his cell phone from the improvised phone holder on the dashboard. The phone began to ring, and after two rings Mary answered.

"Hello," she said sweetly. Her voice was warm and soothing.

"Hi, beautiful," John said quickly.

"Hi, John, I'm so excited!" Without pause she added, "I bought a new dress. I've been saving for it forever. I had my hair done, and now I'm letting my nails dry. I even dieted and lost five pounds this week. Everything's going to be so perfect."

"Mary, I-I," John paused searching for a way to explain. "I didn't know you were looking forward to tonight so much. I ... well, I ... I forgot. I'm in Arkansas."

"What? You're not serious. John, you promised!" She began to cry. She was truly, deeply disappointed. "This is the second time this month that you've had something come up!"

Her voice cracked and she began to sob. "It's just not fair, John!" She paused, and John was at a loss for words. She was right. "Where are you, anyway?" she asked.

"I'm on the road to Marked Tree, Arkansas, then I'm on my way to Missouri to the reservation. Old Bear Daddy called me today. You remember me telling you about him?"

"Yes," she said, trying to hold back further tears.

"Bear Daddy and his grandson discovered a cave that's never been explored. Well, not in recent years, anyway. It has wall drawings, symbols . . . the works! This might be one of the biggest finds in North America this century. Apparently a rockslide or minor tremor has just exposed the entrance. It's really big, Mary."

Silence was all that he heard.

"Are you still there? What do you think?"

Silence again.

"Mary?"

Silence. It felt to John that the whole world was holding its breath.

The smart phone indicated that Mary had not hung up, but no sound could be heard. There was not any crying or even the slightest hushed breathing. John knew this was not good.

"Let me tell you what is big, John." Mary, with new resolve, took a deep breath. "This is big. I'm sick and tired of being stood up, forgotten about, and being alone. Do you hear? Alone! I'm not going to let you do this to me again. I've worked all week and looked forward to seeing you and having a good time together, and here you go again. Once again! You need to decide what's more important—your adventures or me! Don't bother calling. Goodbye, John."

She immediately hung up the phone, not waiting for, or really wanting, a reply. She was angry and disappointed.

John stared at the phone in a daze. He was completely shocked. She had never acted like this before. Mary had always been so forgiving, so understanding. Women were a complete mystery to him. *She'll calm down,* he thought to himself. *I hope.*

He dialed again, but no answer. The phone just rang and rang.

John shut off his smart phone and started down the long, dark, empty road in the direction of Poplar Bluff.

He suddenly felt more alone than he had ever felt before. He had a very hollow feeling throughout his whole body. What if she really didn't want him in her life anymore? Why had she acted this way? He just didn't understand why she was so upset! He might be headed toward a once-in-a-lifetime discovery. This could make his career overnight. Why, he had even thought about asking her to marry him when he graduated. But now he may have missed his chance. His stomach began to feel queasy, and he couldn't understand it, but he felt nauseated. What if she started dating someone else? She was very pretty. Beautiful, in fact.

I'll make it up to her, he told himself. John tried her number again, but by now he was out of range of the cell phone tower. He would just have to try again later when he got to the reservation. *I love her. I really can't stand to be without her!* he thought with a new misery.

After another two hours at the wheel, he arrived at his destination. The gate was really just a place where the road passed between two poles, connected at the top with an arch. Within the arch was framed a sign that posted the reservation name. There was an asphalt parking lot close by, surrounded by tall loblolly pines, where he could settle down for the night. Once parked, he tried Mary's number again; it rang and rang, but no answer. John's stomach twisted up again.

He got out and opened up the hatch on the back of the truck and pulled out the tarpaulin, the folding table, and three lawn chairs, in front of which he set a small, screened, metal fire pit. John put a bundle of hickory firewood onto the pit and lit it with his Bic lighter. He reached into his cooler and brought out an ice-cold bottle of water, a bag of cold cuts, wheat bread, pickles, lettuce, and brown mustard that he had packed earlier.

John then made a sandwich, ate it, and decided to call Mary again. Maybe she had calmed down by now, and he could get back in her good favor before he would see her in Memphis, Monday morning.

The smartphone sprang to life again, and within seconds was ringing Mary's number. This time, after four rings, a recording requested him to leave a message or a number. Conners felt uneasy, but left a message, saying that he was sorry and would call again. He then busied himself with setting up camp for the night. The tarp he carried was one that he had crafted to work as a stand-alone tent or it could be connected by grommets and a nylon rope to the open tailgate and hatch of his truck. He had a small solar panel and battery setup that operated a light and handheld radio and provided a charge for his laptop computer and smartphone. His surplus army cot and blanket set inside the truck's bed gave him a comfortable place to sleep.

With the tent set up, Conners pulled out his leather-bound journal, sat at his portable table with Coleman lantern glowing, and began to write down all the things that had happened during the day. Most of the entries were just like all those found on hundreds of pages before, but as he got toward the end of the day he paused. Then he wrote, "Mary really got mad at me today. I forgot that I had promised to take her out. I really did not understand that it was so important to her. I tried to call and apologize, but I can't reach her."

John began to imagine her having fun on a date with someone else. Maybe she took another man to see *Macbeth*. It was horrible. How could he have taken her so much for granted? He wished now that he had not eaten anything. His stomach was feeling sick again.

Mary was not one to be dramatic unless there was good reason. What if she had really had enough of his not showing up, or being late, or forgetting? Now he remembered all the birthdays, holidays, and other special occasions—too many to count—that she had endured him forgetting. She was right. He simply must change.

He wrote in the journal, "MUST CHANGE."

His thoughts drifted for a moment. He and Mary always had fun together. John had never really thought about any other girl but Mary. The knot in his heart tightened. He loved her.

He wrote in capital letters, "I MUST CHANGE AND SAY I'M SORRY AND REALLY MEAN IT."

With that written, he closed the journal and put it away. He then put up the rest of his gear. John closed the chain curtain at the rear of the truck, set his alarm, and turned in for the night.

It was cool in the mountains at this time of night and this time of year. Here, there was a different feeling from the Delta of Mississippi. The Delta has an indescribable feeling to it at night. The air is heavy with humidity and softly warm. John laid back and thought about the haunting romantic feeling that he always had in the Delta when he and Mary sat outside and watched the moon rise. John said his prayers and quickly went to sleep.

By five thirty that next morning, the alarm buzzed and John rolled over and fell out of the cot onto the truck bed with a thud.

"Ugh!" he moaned, as he rubbed his sleep-fused eyes.

He quickly dressed, made coffee, started breakfast, and reset the chairs and table under the tent so he could accommodate his old friends when they arrived.

In less than half an hour, the chief pulled up.

"Bear Daddy!" Conners yelled out when he saw the chief drive through the gate. "Come over and have a seat."

"Hello, Conners."

John made a wide, sweeping gesture toward the chairs in the shade of the tent. A small campfire burned in the fire pit and chased away the early morning dampness. The pleasant smells of breakfast were starting to waft from the pit. Conners then reached to shake Bear Daddy's outstretched hand. They both sat down with smiles on their faces.

"Coffee?"

"Yes, Conners, I'd like a cup. You look like you are doing well."

"I am. And you look fit as ever."

"I walk a lot through these hills and valleys; it's my way. The countryside makes me happy. How about you? Do you have a good woman yet? Married?"

"No. Not yet."

"You need a good woman to make you happy, Conners," the old chief looked him in the eye and winked. "Will keep you calm ."

"I know. I'm not doing so well in that department right now, Chief. My girlfriend is mad at me, but I'm hoping we will get back together soon."

Then John smiled and said, "Hope you don't mind. I took the liberty to invite our friend, Mark, to meet us here. He loves to help, and is an expert spelunker."

"Oh, that's great," said Bear Daddy. "I remember him from our last visit. He's a good explorer. It will be good to see him again."

"That's him now!" John exclaimed as Mark pulled his Land Rover next to the entrance gate, got out, and waved hello.

"Glad you could meet us here, Mark. Would you like some breakfast? Coffee? Bacon? Eggs? The biscuits are canned, but they are hot."

"Sure. Coffee first. Bear Daddy, I've missed getting to talk with you. How's the family?"

"Great, Mark. My grandson is growing by leaps and bounds."

"I'm sure he is. He was just knee-high when I saw him several years ago. I hope I get to see him on this trip. So, tell us about the cave."

"Well my grandson and I were out yesterday walking through the woods. He noticed a rockslide on a steep mountain wall. It turned out to be a new opening in the mountainside. Inside we found a large crack in the cave's floor. It seemed to have no bottom, and on the cave walls there were drawings like nothing that I had ever seen before or heard of anywhere around these parts. This, I think, is our sacred ancestral cave that has been lost to us for many generations. The story of the cave is one of our legends."

"That's fantastic!" John exclaimed. "Bear Daddy, I couldn't wait to get over here. We just made a big discovery in a site over in the Mississippi Delta. I think it may be connected to Native Americans in the southeast corner of Missouri, right where your people live, and there is reference to a large cave, too!"

The three men looked at each other with growing interest in the coincidence of two similarly important discoveries.

"I remember one time you told me that the use of bear in your name came from a tradition of the chiefs all honoring the tribe's protector bear sent by the Great Spirit. Am I remembering correctly?"

"Yes. Yes, you are right, John. The belief goes back more generations than I can recite. It involved a gigantic cave and a gigantic bear that had spiritual powers."

"Bear Daddy, why didn't you ever mention the cave?"

"I didn't really know that it truly existed until this week, and I didn't think you would believe the fantastical elements of the story. It seems so strange and unusual … well, until now. I am named for the bear spirit. We have stories of a warrior and a great, long cave that stretches for hundreds of miles to the great waters of the north. The stories are very old. Many times, whole generations of our people were wiped out in our tribe, leaving only small numbers to remember. The stories change and many details fade, change, or disappear. We will now know if they are accurate."

"I'll bet the stories are mostly right, Bear Daddy!"

John proceeded to relate the ancient legend, as he understood it from the old explorer's journal. When he had finished, Bear Daddy was completely astounded. "That closely matches our history as handed down to me."

John shook his head in wonder.

"John, let me also fill you and Mark in on the problems that my tribe and I have been going through lately."

Mark shifted in his chair to better hear Bear Daddy.

"Last year, our tribe entered some early talks with a company known as Big Deal, Incorporated. They have done developments for several Native American tribes across the United States and have had some good, and some bad, commercial results. They say they will develop the infrastructures in our area, for example, schools, fire protection, community centers, and healthcare facilities. My nephew is strongly in favor of their proposals. He has a following, mostly of young adults. Of course, all this is good to them, but what they don't say is that somewhere along the way, our culture and natural settings will be lost forever, as will our autonomy."

Mark and John nodded their heads solemnly, empathizing with the older man's dilemma.

"The company is very aggressive. Without our permission, they sent a survey team of two men onto our property last year. The worst thing happened. The team was lost in the wilderness, and no trace of them was ever found. Rumors began, I think started by someone at Big Deal Construction, which seemed to indicate that I might have had something to do with their disappearance."

John's mouth dropped.

"I had nothing to do with it, and no evidence was ever found against me, but it does look bad because I have been against all the proposals that the company has made so far. The owner of the company is trying to turn my people against me. We do need all the advantages of the development, but our people must own our land and keep our ways, or we will become invisible and the Great Spirit will never recognize us again."

Mark rubbed his chin thoughtfully.

"I've been targeted, John. Someone tried to kill my grandson and me yesterday by cutting the brake line on my truck. I have no doubt the construction company had a hand in it. They don't want me to speak against them at our next tribal meeting. The company will be there, as will most of the voting members of our tribe. I don't know what will happen."

John and Mark offered Bear Daddy their support in fighting these unfounded rumors and suggested he take extra precautions for his safety, at least until this conflict was resolved.

Bear Daddy shook his head. "Anyway, let's get y'all to the cave."
"I can't wait!" John said.
"Me, either!" added Mark.

THE CAVE—FIRST VISIT

THE THREE MEN FINISHED BREAKFAST, CLEANED UP, AND drove together to the site.

"Let's take these backpacks and flashlights," John said. "I also have three lanterns; like the Boy Scouts, I stay prepared. You never know when you'll get just one chance to make a discovery. Everyone needs to grab one full spool of comeback nylon cord. We never can be too careful."

They walked down the quiet mountain trail. The trees were huge, mature, and majestic. They towered above the men like silent sentinels, guarding a secret passage. The gentle sounds of the forest engulfed the explorers. Clean, fresh air swept across the ancient path. In the distance, they saw the newly disturbed rocky rubble at the end of the trail.

A whooping crane called woefully for its mate in the distance. For a while, they walked on in silence, each one lost in his private world, taking in the timeless beauty of the woods. Soon they came to the cave entrance. The area was overgrown with a thick covering of brush.

"Looks good," John said. "The opening is really fresh."

"Do you think it's safe?" Mark asked.

"Don't know, but the inner walls look good from here. There is such thick brush here it's hard to be sure."

"Smells musty and wet, but don't they all."

"There must be water, and the inside hasn't been exposed for quite a while," John said. "Attach your cord and light your lanterns, men. We'll hope we don't have any more aftershocks around here until we get out."

The loose gravel on the cave floor crunched under their boots as they walked forward. An occasional drop of water splashed ahead, flashing a reflection in the beams of their lights.

John looked back to the opening. The light filtered in through the bright, fall-colored leaves of the forest. The colors were beautiful against the stark contrast of the dark, rocky walls and floor of the cave's interior.

As they went deeper into the cave, the outside light illuminated the space less and less.

"Back here! The wall!" Mark exclaimed. Mark set his lantern down at the base of the wall. The three men gazed in silence at a half-dozen pictures drawn on the wall showing a great bear with a paw missing one claw.

"This is terrific!" John said.

"Like my tribe's old stories!" Bear Daddy said.

"Look over there! It appears to be a pool. It's crystal clear and seems to be very deep, too. I'll bet it comes out under that rock wall over there." John pointed.

"That probably goes to another part of this cave deeper in the mountain," Mark said.

"Yes, it probably does," John replied. "I've seen these pools run for hundreds of yards and go under rock and open into other caves. We can come back with scuba gear and explore next time."

"Yeah! This is an old place. I think that your tribe must have come here for hundreds of years. No telling what we'll find, Bear Daddy!"

"Yes, John, finding the opening to the cave is a sign to me from the spirit world. I believe the Great Spirit has allowed me to notice this cave. What it holds will save my people and our land from outsiders."

"Yes, Bear Daddy, I understand," John said. "We'll be most careful not to disturb this site as we look for the history that it holds."

The chief patted John on the shoulder with confidence and appreciation for his reverence of history and other people's sacred objects.

"Bear Daddy, I brought my camera. Is it OK to get a few shots of this wall?"

"Yes, John Conners, you always show respect for our people. It will be good for you to research this place and help my people understand how it relates to us."

John began to photograph the wall and made certain he included all the drawings, the chamber, and the pool.

"We might be able to put this place on the National Register. If we could, there would be no Construction Destruction!" John chuckled aloud, tickled by his clever play on words.

"Your mountain would be safe," clarified Mark more seriously, as he spoke to Bear Daddy.

At that thought, Bear Daddy went to his knees. He was absolutely overtaken by the importance of the moment. He raised his hands skyward and began an ancient chant. His tones grew louder and then softer. Over and over he thanked the Great Spirit.

"This is truly a special place," John remarked. Mark nodded in agreement.

"Check out the direction of this crack in the cave floor, Mark. See what your compass reads."

Mark held the compass over the map. He quickly ran his index finger over an imaginary direction and he stopped.

"Memphis! And this other is in the direction of St. Louis!"

"You're right. It also matches the wall painting. There were no cities when this was painted but all the topography matches."

"Look behind you. That must represent the Mississippi River."

Mark turned.

"And look, higher, I'll bet that spot is where present-day St. Louis sits!"

Mark waved the flashlight to the wall and, although crude, there was no question that the charcoal lines went right toward the place in the drawing of the river where Memphis, Tennessee, is located today. "There were Native Americans settled at that place, long ago, along the river bluff. The other lines ran to the area where St. Louis lies today. Both these cities, from looking at this wall painting, would appear to be in great danger from earthquake activity the way it was drawn."

Then the cave shook. A deep rumbling sound blasted through the cave. Overhead rocks crumbled and cascaded down the walls. The crack in the cave floor shuddered and opened inches wider. Seconds later.... Silence. Dust clouds rose up, causing all in the cave to cough and gasp for breath.

"This thing is definitely active. We should get outside for now," warned Mark.

The men made a hurried retreat, stopping at the cave entrance. "Let's talk to the people at the Center for Earthquake Research and Information at the University of Memphis. They can help us with all this information," John said. "They have access to high-rate GPS, geodetic dating, and seismology. Intra and inter plate deformation in the whole New Madrid area."

"Let's block off the entrance. Don't tell anyone about the exact location of the cave entrance yet. We don't want any looting or damage. This may save your land, Bear Daddy. The value of this land as a National Park with all its history could be much greater than any profits a casino could bring. If it's OK, we'll start to explore this cave completely as soon as possible," John asked of Bear Daddy.

"That would be good, John."

The three walked out, covering the entrance with leafy tree branches before making their way back to the gate. John and Mark searched their calendars for a return date to explore with scuba equipment. Both men were very busy this time of year and fitting something, even this important, into both schedules proved very difficult.

"Seven weeks from now, on Friday?"

They all nodded in agreement.

John and Mark left for Memphis. They sped, one following the other, through the warm fall afternoon, over the winding, narrow, country roads through the quiet of Missouri and then the Arkansas countryside.

So many secrets lay beneath the soil, John thought. *History is right here to be understood and waiting for someone to make sense of it all.*

What an opportunity we have to learn from the experiences of others in times past and benefit from their knowledge!

The two friends arrived in Memphis, gestured their farewells, and then went back to their respective homes.

McTavish, John's West Highland White Terrier, greeted him happily. "At least someone is happy with me, pup!" John said softly, as he patted the excited dog. "Come on in, little fellow. You've had a long time in your outdoor kennel. You may stay inside tonight. There's no sense in us both being lonely."

Later that night, John tried, once again, to reach Mary on the phone. He could hear the phone ring over and over again, but there was no response. He would see her Monday and try to change her mind about… well, about everything.

John decided to call Mark.

"I just wanted to let you know that I'll call sometime Monday and make sure we can get the scuba equipment."

"Sure, just let me know. I'll get my gear together. The pool in the cave may be very deep."

"I surely hope so. That will make for a greater chance for connection with another chamber."

"Yeah. It just worries me a little about the possibility of an earthquake. What do you think?"

"I don't know. It's the right place for one. Everything that I've ever read about the New Madrid Fault says that the cycle is over five hundred years and the last one was in 1812. We should be able to take a chance. But you never know. The cave has survived up till now. I think we will be fine."

"I'm ready."

"Good. Nothing ventured, nothing gained, right? I'll call you later this week to set up a time of day for the next meeting."

Later that night at his apartment, John tuned in, as usual, to Channel Five Evening News. Jack Jennings, the broadcaster, went over the events of the day. He and Mark and Jack had gone to undergraduate school at the University of Mississippi together. They were the best of friends in college. But after graduation, they seldom saw Jack, except on television, of course.

John sat down at his desk and started to pull up maps and other information about Arkansas, Missouri, Native American tribes, and the history of the area. The University of Memphis had quite a bit of information available about the New Madrid Fault and a wealth of data on earthquakes in the Memphis area. A team of geologists independently studied the activity of the earth in the area and had posted some of their findings. One of the most interesting articles that John found was about a Native American named Tecumseh.

According to legend, Tecumseh predicted the 1812 earthquake over a year in advance. How did he do it? What gave him the ability? Was the story of the prediction really true? *If only we could predict earthquakes,* John mused, *so many lives and so much property could be saved.*

John went from site to site looking for information. He sat on his sofa with his laptop for hours researching every lead.

Was the bear head pottery a coincidence? Could the cave in Missouri and the site he had excavated in Mississippi be connected? Possibly. He was lost in deep thought about the new cave for hours. Could this be Manapah's cave and bear? Bear Daddy certainly thought so.

John went to the kitchen and made a tall glass of sweet tea. Then he went into his second bedroom that he used as an office, library, and study. He settled into his favorite desk chair, put his feet up on his old metal desk, and rocked back in his chair.

All of a sudden, he was gripped by the silence like a vise, by the starkness of the room in the apartment. He felt small and alone.

Mary, he thought. *I miss you.*

As he sat there, he became aware of the paddles on the ceiling fan slowly turning around and around, never going anywhere. With each turn, the wind from the paddles seemed to say, "Mary, Mary, Mary."

I've got to talk to her, he thought.

John looked at his clock radio. The illuminated display brightly showed the time was eleven o'clock.

"It's Saturday night, too! I completely forgot. I'm driving to her apartment right now! No, wait. I'll call first. She may not be home," he said to himself. The thought of her out with another man horrified him. "I've got to know!" he exclaimed, as he pushed the button to speed-dial her number.

The phone rang four times before it went to voicemail. "Mary here. Hello, I can't answer now, but leave a message at the tone. Bye for now."

"Mary, I've got to talk to you. I am truly sorry. I've acted badly... Well, anyway, please let me meet you Monday between lectures, or better yet, tomorrow! Mark and I made some great discoveries in Missouri. I know you'll be interested. I-I love you, Mary. Please meet me tomorrow. Call me back and tell me where and I'll be there. Bye."

John felt sad and lonely, sadder than he had ever felt in his whole life. He knew he would have to wait to see her on campus Monday.

John had no way of knowing that earlier that day Richard Clark had called Mary. He had called many times before, but Mary had always declined his offers for a date because she and John were an item. Not anymore.

Richard was pleasantly surprised when Mary answered. Richard proceeded to ask her to go to the Orpheum theater production of *Oklahoma*. She happily accepted his offer. Mary was pleased to be escorted by one of the most eligible bachelors in west Tennessee. Her new dress and carefully done nails would get a proper outing.

Richard was a successful Memphis businessman. He contributed heavily to the University of Memphis and was a very popular civic leader. As the son of a well-to-do family, he virtually walked into the family business at the top when his father died early in life of a heart attack.

Richard knew the construction business well. His projects were large and so were the profits. The company had grown quickly under his command. Richard was cutting corners at every chance in the construction of new buildings, and he was becoming more ruthless with the bidding of each new contract.

Mary and Richard had a good time at the play. Although he was pleasant to be around, Mary still caught herself thinking of John.

At the end of the evening, Mary bid Richard farewell at her front door with a handshake.

When Mary was inside her apartment, she played her phone messages.

"Another message from John," she said out loud. "Humph, I'm going to move on. Move on!"

But as she folded her arms across her chest, a pang of sentiment swept across her. She heard herself softly say, "I do love him …but I'm not going to call him back!"

John got to the staff parking lot early Monday morning. He stopped on the way and picked up coffee and the donuts that he knew Mary liked best. Latte and cream-filled donuts for her, and American coffee and plain glazed donuts for himself.

When Mary drove up, John gave her a terrific wave. She saw him, but popped her head back in the car. With her left hand, she flipped her hair to cover the left side of her face to shield her view of John. Pretending not to notice him, she busied herself with picking up and arranging papers on the front seat of her car.

Not to be discouraged, John walked up to her partially opened car door. "Hi, I brought you your favorite morning snack … Peace offering?" He smiled.

Mary pushed out her lower jaw. Her eyebrows converged. "Mister Conners, what makes you think that you can sweet-talk and bribe me? Do you think that I'm that shallow and easy?"

"No, of course not, but I thought we might … well, start over. This time I would be more thoughtful and caring." John flashed a sheepish, but winning smile at her.

He *is so irresistible when he smiles*, she thought.

John nudged the peace offering just slightly in Mary's direction.

"Well, OK. I'm Mary Morrow, pleased to meet you."

"The feeling's mutual. I'm John Conners. May I offer you a coffee and donut?"

"Yes, that would be lovely."

Mary tried to hold back a smile, but it burst forth betraying her true feelings. Only the corners of her mouth turned up and her nose crinkled just a little. John saw it, and a twinkle came to his eyes. He knew this was the girl that he would always love.

"So, what were you doing this weekend, John?" Mary asked.

"Chief Bear Daddy called last week. He found a cave on the reservation. An earthquake tremor opened it up last week. He begged me to come explore it with him. A gaming company is trying to railroad a deal with his people to build a casino right in the middle of his pristine reservation. He thought something about this cave might be important enough to save the place. He was desperate. The good news is I think he might be right—the cave seems to be remarkably important. Mark and I went with him and explored the cave. The cave has paintings on the walls that match his tribe's oldest legends and coincide with the information that we just discovered in the journal we found at our dig site in the Mississippi Delta . . . the one you helped me decipher."

"Wow, that's big!"

"Well, I was supposed to meet with Mark last Saturday down at the Delta dig, so I just changed the location to Missouri, instead. It was a much longer drive, but it was worth it. We met Bear Daddy at the reservation, went to the cave, and photographed the wall paintings. There was a large pool of water in the cave that may lead to a larger chamber. We are going to get scuba gear together and meet back there and see where the pool leads. Hopefully, it will open up deeper into the mountain and into more chambers. We think the cave was originally dry and later filled with water."

Mary took a sip of her latte, at a loss for words at his wondrous news.

"And there's something else. The cave paintings seem to warn about a massive earthquake ... seems to be a warning about a really big one. There are what appear to be constellation drawings and other celestial markers in the mix, but we need time to figure out their meaning."

"Everyone knows about the New Madrid Fault, John," Mary said.

"I know, I know, but this seems to show a way to predict the quake. There's something about these drawings. I just know it. The cave floor also has a huge crack running through it. I mean, it's big enough to drop an eighteen-wheeler into it and never see it again."

"John, that sounds fantastic! Are you going to tell people about this? You'll have to be careful about the way you present this information."

"I know. It does sound a little crazy! I'm going to call Jack Jennings and see if he will interview Mark and me on his news show. Actually, we can't reveal the exact location yet, because there is so much at stake. Legal matters can go on forever. I just want safety measures in place. At the same time, I feel any time we wait to get prepared for the earthquake is time wasted."

"That's very well thought out, John."

"I'm also going to go to the mayor's office and talk to him about raising public awareness in regard to earthquakes."

"John, those are excellent plans."

"Say, if you can, I'd like you to join me for Bear Daddy's tribal meeting next weekend. He's going to present his opinions to the tribe about the development of the reservation, and the other side will present their arguments. The tribe will have to decide whether or not to allow the casino to build on the reservation. There will be a vote, and this vote should settle the future for the tribe. Bear Daddy will only state his case based on his thoughts. We can't mention the cave yet until we know more about it. The precise location is secret for now because we don't want looting. We need a couple more months to be able to present an argument regarding the cave. Hopefully, for Bear Daddy's sake, the government will then deem it a National Shrine on a reservation. Then no one could build near the cave, no matter what the outcome of the vote is. Watching how a tribal meeting is held should prove interesting. Do you want to go with me?"

"Sure, it sounds interesting. Can't wait!"

THROW YOUR BEST PITCH

THE NEXT DAY JOHN SAT AT HIS HOME OFFICE DESK IN his small apartment. McTavish lay beside him on the floor, nestled in his fluffy, plaid pillow. John scrolled down the list of names and numbers on his cell phone and stopped when he came to Jack Jennings, known as JJ by his best friends, and dialed his number.

"JJ, John Conners here. How are you?"

"Hello, John. Doing great! It's been a while."

"Yes, it has. Too long. I catch your show on Channel Five a couple of nights a week. You're doing a great job."

"Thanks."

"JJ, does your TV station still let you do special interest spots?"

"Yes, we get calls all the time, screen them, and if the material is good, we put it on the air. Do you have something in mind?"

"Yes, I do. I got a call from a friend of mine the other day. He's the chief of a Native American tribe and lives on a reservation in southeast Missouri. Some tremors in the area opened up a new cave

62

entrance, and we found what appears to be very early cave paintings on the walls."

"That's great material, John. I'd be happy to work that up. Tell me more about it."

"The cave is in danger of being destroyed by a land development company. The tribe is close to being persuaded to develop the area for a casino complex. There's a big vote coming up in a tribal meeting over whether or not to allow the company to proceed with its plans. The chief is against the idea, but his young nephew is leading a group that's all for it. There is a lot of confusion and hard feelings developing.

"I also have some geological and earthquake data that would be good to go over about the area. There is, possibly, some connection of this cave to the New Madrid Fault. There are writings on the cave walls that indicate fault lines. The chief seems to think it has something to do with the prediction Tecumseh made of the 1812 earthquake. If the construction destroys the cave, we will possibly have ruined a great chance to predict when another earthquake will occur. Until we can make better predictions, I strongly feel we all need to be prepared. When can we get together and go over the information?" John asked.

"Well, the TV station was sent complementary tickets to the Redbird's post-season inter-squad game tonight. The proceeds go to charity, to Saint Jude's, I think. We could go over everything there."

"Great! Look, do you think we could get an extra ticket? Mark McKenzie is exploring the cave with me."

"Sure, I'll meet you and Mark tonight at the stadium at seven o'clock. We all had some great times at the baseball games in Oxford when we were in college. It'll be like old times."

That evening, the temperature dropped down to the low sixties. There was a clear sky and just a slight wind coming from the southwest. Downtown Memphis was full of people, out to have a good time. AutoZone stadium was filling up with fans.

"Jack!" Mark shouted, as he walked up to the front of the stadium entrance. "Good to see you again."

"You too, Mark," Jack replied as he extended his hand to shake Mark's.

"John!" Jack called, as he spotted John coming around the corner and approaching them. "Over here!"

The three men, in their early thirties, talked about what they had been doing since they left college as they waited in line to get into the game. The stadium was nearly full, and the mood of the crowd was high.

"Well, John, what have you been doing?"

"I finished with a masters in Anthropology at Ole Miss and got a position with the Mississippi Archeological Service. I worked for the state full time until now. They allowed me to take a part-time job while I pursue a Ph.D. at the University of Memphis. I'm teaching there also. Dr. Jean Woodman is the chair of the department. She's tough, but fair. I have directed excavations at several Native American earth mounds and village sites. The service does work with volunteers from all the surrounding universities, and there's a great deal of travel involved." John added.

"Are you still dating that beautiful girl? Ah…Mary?"

"Yes! Well, I think I am. We had a little misunderstanding. Actually, I'm worried I may have messed up bad, but I am trying to patch things up as best I can."

"I would do that soon, John. That's a great girl."

"You're right, JJ. I just didn't realize that she was so serious."

"They're all serious when it comes to relationships," quipped JJ.

"And you, Mark?" JJ asked.

"Well, I've worked in finance with several companies and got a great position with a terrific investment company here in Memphis. I get to travel and work with some wonderful people. Plus, I'd say that I get adequate time off work." Mark smiled and did a "thumbs up" gesture.

"Mark, is your wife still in medical school?" Jack asked.

"Graduated. She's an OB/GYN resident here at the university hospital. She's working full time now, but I don't know how long she can manage that schedule. She's seven months pregnant and is having a tough time. She's been working so hard delivering other people's babies that she almost lost ours. Her doctor wants her to take it easy and get back to her full-time routine later. I'm really happy that she told her that, because I don't think she would cut back on her own. I have been really worried about her."

"Oh, I'm sorry to hear that, Mark. I sincerely hope for the best for her. Well, for all three of you," Jack said sincerely.

Three! thought Mark as he pondered the very sound of a family of three.

"John, tell me about your new find," JJ implored, as he turned away from Mark, who was obviously not thinking about the cave anymore. "I could tell when you called me that you were really excited about it. I haven't had a chance to be involved in something outside of work here at the news station for a long time."

"The site is spectacular, but I've got other worries, and my thoughts may sound far-fetched," John said. "I'm really concerned about the possibility of a massive earthquake in the New Madrid

Fault area. The cave that my friend, Bear Daddy, found has huge fissures in it and they are absolutely fresh. There have been new steam vents developing in several places on his reservation and new pools of hot water, where there were never any before between the reservation and Memphis. Hot Springs, Arkansas has always had hot pools and vents, but this is the first area this far north that has had them. The people at CERI told us that the changes are significant, but they can't make a call. on a possible earthquake event. CERI was created at the University of Memphis in 1977. They keep up with earthquake activity around the world. GPS and seismic networks are monitored and research on prediction and preparedness are carried out and are available to the public.." . John continued. .

"John, come on! Do you still write for that struggling magazine, ah, what is it ... *Explorers Unlimited*? You're not trying to set up some spectacular background for a lead story, are you?"

"No, No! Jack, I'd never do that! I do think several big events are about to happen, though. This really is about a struggle of a people to preserve their culture and protect the natural beauty of the area where they live, but at the same time, move into a modern world where they may have a better future.

"The future? Maybe you are overreaching here a bit," Jack said, skeptically.

"There is a battle going on between the tribe, the casino development company, and between different factions in the tribe. At stake, isn't just the tribe's social future, but the preservation of an important piece of land that may hold secrets about the future of our continent. Yes, it is big, but it's not overreaching. It would be an interesting story for your news show, Jack. I'd like to try to get enough attention to this issue so the development company can't railroad a deal that will destroy the countryside or take advantage of the people. The other thing of course is to alert the people of Memphis to the possibility of an earthquake happening … maybe soon! If this cave is as informative as we think it may be, we could possibly predict an earthquake with some accuracy. It simply *cannot* be destroyed. We need to keep it safe until we have studied it."

"That does sound interesting, and important to a lot of people," Jack said. "I would like to get the particulars and do a photoshoot with them. Do you think you can set it up? Could I interview you on my show so you could relay your beliefs to the public without getting anyone upset at the station or with me?" asked JJ.

"Yes," John agreed. "That's a great idea. Let's set it up."

"That's a good way to handle it. I'd like to look at the data you have and go over the show with you. We could work up some interest with the people and, maybe, help motivate the city to make more serious preparations."

"It's going to be a lot of work, but I think it will do a lot of good. Maybe even save lives."

"Strike three!" The umpire thrust his arm into the air, and the batter's arms dropped.

"Hey! This Redbirds pitcher is really good. He has a mean tailing fastball!" Mark said.

"You're right," John agreed.

"I've watched this guy a couple of times. He gets lots of strikeouts. I'm pretty sure we'll see him at the next level soon."

The young men finished watching the game and agreed to do an interview on Jack's TV show on Wednesday night at ten o'clock.

As they were about to leave the ballpark, Mark's smartphone sprang to life.

"It's happening again. I'm still at the hospital!" Marissa said.

"What's the matter, Mark?" John asked as he saw his friend's face turn white.

"It's Marissa. She feels like she's in labor again. I've got to get to the hospital quickly. See you Wednesday night."

Mark rushed to the Baptist Women's hospital and found Marissa in an emergency room cubical.

"Honey, how are you?"

"Ohhh," she moaned, as she concentrated on her breathing. "Oh, they're going to check me in a few minutes to see if I'm dilated," Marissa said between labored breaths. "This feels like the real thing. Sorry I had to call. Did you miss any of the game?"

"No, hun. It really isn't important. Everything's all right. We're going to do a spot about the controversy at the reservation and a warning about earthquakes on Jack's ten o'clock show, on Wednesday."

"Great." Marissa managed a smile, but then the waves of pain came back. "Oh!"

Mark went to her bedside and kissed her on the forehead. "Are you OK?"

"Yes, yes. It's just cramping. I'll be fine. OH! OH! Here it comes again!" Marissa screamed. *Correction. This is not just cramping,* Marissa thought to herself.

The attending physician came in and examined Marissa.

"You're OK," he said. "It's false labor. I know it feels like the real thing, but as you know, it's just your body preparing you for when it is the real thing. You'll be fine. We'll keep you here overnight, but don't worry. You are fine."

Miraculously, Marissa suddenly felt better after the diagnosis and was able to speak more easily. "Mark, why don't you and your friends talk to the mayor of Memphis? You may be able to convince him that additional investment in preparing for an earthquake is necessary and worthwhile, even if it is probably going to be years before one really occurs. You know, an ounce of prevention—"

"Yeah, you're right. John mentioned it, too. I'll check with his office and see if we can meet him tomorrow. I'm off a few days, and it would be great to get his thoughts on this situation before we are interviewed on *News at Ten*," Mark added.

The next morning, Marcus Lamont, the Mayor of Memphis, agreed to talk to Mark and John. It was unusual to get to speak with the mayor on such short notice, but time was available thanks to a last-minute cancellation of an appointment someone else had had with Mr. Lamont. The mayor was a big man. His height was six feet, seven inches. He had an athletic build and had majored in city planning in college. He went to law school and graduated Summa Cum Laude from Vanderbilt University, where he was enrolled as DeMarcus Lamont. He was the third African-American mayor of Memphis and was responsible for unprecedented business growth and a period of harmony among the Memphis residents, which was the hope of all surrounding communities.

"Hello, gentlemen. I'm Mayor Lamont. I've heard that you guys are worried about the future of our fair city."

"Yes, we wanted to talk with you about being prepared for a major earthquake," Mark said.

"I see. Well, let's hear your concerns," the Mayor of Memphis said and smiled.

"We suspect a major earthquake is about to happen," John began. "We've been investigating a cave. There has been seismic activity there. The area between the cave and Memphis has developed hot water pools and actual fissures in bedrock in the direction of Memphis. There are also in this cave ancient paintings, depicting a great catastrophe. This could be a warning for an earthquake in our area."

"Well, when is this quake going to occur?" asked the mayor.

"We don't know exactly. It could be now or maybe years from now. We're not sure. We just wanted to alert the city to the possibility, maybe try to get the fire and police departments ready."

"We have been preparing here in Memphis for years," the mayor replied. "You'd have to check with the State of Tennessee, but I'm pretty sure we have geologists who regularly check for radon gas level changes and other alterations in the earth's surface. I don't know, fellas. If I make a public announcement that an earthquake could happen soon, there might be chaos. Some people can be animals in times of crisis. They will become irrational, panic, and maybe kill scores of people. It would be worse than a quake."

Hearing, but basically ignoring, the mayor's concern, Mark sat up straight, then leaned forward, peering into the mayor's eyes and posed these scenarios. "Say if we tried to evacuate Memphis. Where would all the people go? How do you feed and water that many? Shelter would require enormous numbers of tents or mobile homes. If the quake strikes during the winter months, how do we heat these structures? Sanitation: how do we take care of their basic needs?"

Lamont listened, and then made his point again. "If it were a false alarm, I'd lose all my credibility with the people and other government agencies. I don't think so, gentlemen. What I will do is contact FEMA, the federal government agency that is supposed to take care of these kinds of problems, and ask them to provide us with a workable plan for such a situation."

"With respect, Mayor, we already checked into the plan," said Mark. "Known as the Catastrophic Earthquake Disaster Response Planning initiative, the plan is all-inclusive and covers Alabama, Arkansas, Illinois, Indiana, Kentucky, Missouri, Mississippi, and Tennessee. It will be necessary as recovery efforts evolve. However, we think that each population center will be more efficient and effective in the early hours of the disaster response."

"Yes, speed is so important when it comes to rescue," John added.

"Well, I will give it some thought," Mayor Lamont said. "I do thank you both for coming today. Your concern for the city is an asset to our community."

"Thank you, Mayor, we hope we can still suggest some ways to help our chances of survival in case we do have an emergency," said John.

"Why, yes, let me hear your suggestions," the Mayor said. He was about to tell them to set up a future meeting with his assistant when the men jumped in before he had the chance.

"What we do need, Mayor, is to be able to contact police and have the citizens encouraged to get two-way radios, with emergency antennas and back-up battery supplies," Mark said.

John added quickly, "The firemen need to have lots of flexible water hoses. The supply hoses should be on reels that can be spun out over rugged terrain and debris such as might be present if buildings fall into the street."

Not missing a beat, Mark said, "The quake will break water lines. We need to be able to pump water out of the Mississippi River and lakes or ponds, if necessary. Then we would need large water filtration systems to supply lots of clean water for lots of people and animals."

"Hospitals need shortwave radios and really heavy-duty, auxiliary power plants and plenty of fuel," John said. "They should have extra triage supplies and portable treatment facilities to take temporary care of large numbers of people. We need to train all health-care workers to provide emergency primary care in these times of extreme emergencies. Many of these folks in health care have already been taught to start an I.V. and administer first aid, but don't use those skills routinely. The city needs to have port-a-potties that can be quickly deployed if our water and sewer treatment plants go down, so we will not have a contaminated water supply."

"The National Guard needs to have the ability to deploy quickly to prevent riots and looting, and your office should have access to bull dozers and backhoes to quickly move debris off roads to allow emergency vehicles to operate," Mark added. "Helicopters should be available to transport emergency cases to hospitals. We could also use a squadron of camera drones to fly over the city and help co-ordinate rescue operations. Drones could also deliver supplies to hospitals and emergency centers."

"Emergency personnel should have the ability to distribute drinking water. Everyone should have tents, first aid kits, flashlights and maps to enable the survivors to get to aid stations," John finished.

All three men took a pause, and Mark and John looked expectantly at the mayor.

"Yes, certainly, I will be happy to hear any suggestions and I will send you all a condensed version of FEMA's plan as soon as I receive a written copy of it," the mayor said, as he opened the door from his office, indicating the meeting was over.

Later on Wednesday, at 10 P.M.

The Channel Five News broadcast studio was packed full of cameras and electronic equipment, and the people who operated them. The two young men were almost overwhelmed with the environment. Jack told Mark and John to watch for the red light on the main TV camera.

"That light means you're on live TV," Jack said. "Just talk to me like we are sitting in your living room, fellas."

Jack reported the day's news from the teleprompter and then the camera backed away as Jack introduced his guests.

"Tonight we are talking to two concerned citizens," Jack said. "They are worried about potential damage to our city from the New Madrid Fault, and they also have concerns about a Native American tribe in Missouri that we would like to share with our viewers. Let me introduce John Conners, archeologist, and Mark McKenzie, a financial consultant, but most importantly for us, an avid spelunker and explorer."

The camera focused on Mark and John, who both nodded and said quiet hellos.

"Mark and John, tell us about the reservation and cave in southern Missouri."

John and Mark carefully explained the proposed casino development and the pros and cons of the plans.

Then they described the cave and highlighted what they had seen: the fissure in the cave, hot water and steam vents, and the markings indicating the possibility of an earthquake hitting Memphis.

"The chief and his people believe the quake is due this year. They have many legends and stories that seem to point in that direction," Jack said. "John, tell us what to expect if a magnitude seven or higher earthquake strikes Memphis."

Jack's invitation to describe a possible scenario of the aftermath of an earthquake opened the door for Mark and John to say what they really wanted to say. The two guests thought warning the viewers of possible destruction would be a way to alert people to the need for preparation, something they felt was imperative.

"Well, the way buildings are constructed here, in the downtown area, the damage will be major," John said. "Unreinforced brick walls, having no structural steel support, will crumble and fall on people in the street and trap those inside the buildings. The concrete multi-level parking lots will collapse like waffle irons on cars and passengers. One of the few buildings that will probably remain standing is the AutoZone building since it was specially designed to hold up in earthquakes. It's built on a flexible foundation, and the whole building is locked together with metal beams."

"What can we as a city do?" Jack pressed for more information.

Mark broke in. "The city needs to have buildings in the downtown area retro-fitted with metal frames and steel mesh coatings applied to the supporting walls," he said. "The hospitals, police and fire stations, and city government buildings should be upgraded to allow them to work in severe emergency conditions and should have realistic drills to perfect their response in all emergency situations."

"Flexible and redundant water, gas, electrical, and sewer lines should also be installed," John said. "The cost will be high, but better now than after the event. Being prepared could save countless lives and property."

"But aren't we years away from the predicted cycle of New Madrid earthquake activity?" Jack queried.

"Well, theoretically you are right. But Mother Nature does not always act according to our mathematical predictions," Mark said. "It could happen at any moment. And this preparation could be helpful in any number of other natural disasters."

"There you have it folks: Be prepared," Jack said. "That's the message from our guests tonight. Tune in tomorrow for the Channel Five Morning News at seven o'clock."

John and Mark waited until the news show was over and thanked Jack for giving them a chance to present the issues they considered so important. The friends left the studio feeling that they had done their duty.

JJ lived in a riverside condominium, just across from Mud Island. It looked over the Mississippi River and was considered a popular and desirable residential area in the city because of the beautiful views. He was the primary anchor for the morning, the six o'clock, and the evening news shows, five days a week.

On most nights, he went to bed as soon as he came home, in order to be refreshed for the next day.

JJ's phone alarm was set to wake him at five in the morning, but he always woke up a few minutes early, before the alarm rang. It was 4:53 A.M., and as he reached for his cell phone to disengage the alarm, the phone rang.

"JJ?"

"Yes, this is he."

"The boss is raging mad at you over last night's show. He wants you to be in his office before the morning news," Madge said.

"What's wrong, Madge?"

"I don't know exactly, but the mayor woke him up last night on the phone, ranting about the thousands of calls that he received from citizens of Memphis thinking we were about to have an earthquake."

"Oh. Well, I'll be there soon."

This is not the best way to start a morning, he thought, as he quickly dressed for the day.

BORED MEETING

THE MAHOGANY TABLE IN THE BOARD MEETING ROOM was twenty feet long, made from four-inch thick planks. It had been sanded by hand, varnished, and rubbed repeatedly until the finish was of the highest quality. The dark walnut paneling and high ceilings of the large conference room spoke of wealth and power.

Andrew McGuire, now twenty-eight years old, had grown up for the most part without a mother or father. When he was a toddler, his parents were killed in a sudden storm that caused their private plane to crash off Nantucket Island, Massachusetts. Most of Andrew's early memories were of nannies or caretakers whose salaries were provided for by his only uncle and, of course, the family corporation, Big Deal Construction, Inc.

After the accident which took his parents' lives, his uncle, Bob McGuire, managed the business. Most of the time, the company had made great moves and was very productive and successful. The board of directors had been happy with Bob's leadership as chief executive officer.

Andrew's small frame and lack of handsome features, along with no interest in the day-to-day operation of the company, made him unpopular with most of the company executives and the rank-and-file employees. Andrew, however, still dreamed of one day taking control of the company.

Only last week, Andrew sat in the company president's chair and felt the smooth, supple leather, as he enjoyed the feeling of command that sitting at the head of the table gave him. He imagined what it would be like to push his uncle aside and run the board meetings and the company. After all, he had graduated from the Wharton School of Business and knew he could handle the challenge.

Today was the first Thursday of the month, and the company board was scheduled to meet.

Andrew walked briskly into the company building and around to the corner of the lobby where he saw his uncle headed for the elevator, on his way to the meeting.

"Hello, Uncle!" Andrew managed to say.

"Hello, Andrew."

Bob McGuire was a big, barrel-chested man in his mid-sixties. He ate right and exercised enough to keep him in shape for sports and an active lifestyle. His graying hair and tailored suit projected a persona of success and leadership.

Andrew smiled and held the elevator door open for his uncle.

"We should have a good meeting today," Bob said.

"Yes, we need some good news."

"You're right about that, Andrew," Bob said. "You know, this is an important board meeting today."

"Yeah, I heard that we're not showing enough profit on the last project," Andrew replied.

"No one knew that the biggest hurricane this century would rip all our new construction to pieces on the coast!" Bob replied, obviously irritated. "Insurance never covers all the losses. We need the board to back our refinance plan, and hopefully, we'll be able to sell this new project to those Native Americans in Missouri. Andrew, if this deal doesn't fly, we may be forced into bankruptcy."

Andrew shook his head.

"OK, I'll vote with you one more time, but I want a chance to run this company one of these days," Andrew said. "You know that, Uncle. I want the projected plan of my becoming the president in writing. If something should happen to you, I'd need all the documents for transfer of authority in place. And—"

"Not now, boy! I don't feel like arguing with you about that! We'll discuss it later."

In an attempt to smooth things over, Andrew decided to change the subject. "Have you been scuba diving lately? I have a great trip planned to the Bahamas next month. I wanted to—"

Bob interrupted. "I haven't done that since last year. Too busy trying to keep this business afloat."

The two men rode the rest of the way in silence. At the top floor of the building, the elevator stopped and the doors opened. Both men smiled mechanically and walked into the meeting. There were already ten other board members in the room. Bob greeted everyone, making eye contact, shaking hands, and smiling at each person. Bob was always great with people and truly enjoyed his role. He went to the head of the table and, with his gavel, called the meeting to order. The group quickly dispensed with the minutes and went straight to the most pressing issues.

"The government has given us a great opportunity," Bob said. "Money in the form of guaranteed low interest loans is to be made available to construction companies and Native American groups on reservations to build entertainment and casino businesses to help lower their unemployment and provide free enterprise opportunities to stimulate the economy. Andrew, what do you think of our chances with the Quan Pawtee people?"

"I think we must get a contract."

Bob continued. "The proposal is a good one, and it will help them out immensely. However, not all of them see it that way. You know we've already talked to the old chief. He's standing in the way. I don't know if we can persuade them that our plans are best for their people. We have charts and videos of what we've done for other tribes on other reservations.

"We have many from the tribe who are on our side and who want to use this opportunity to benefit their community. The old chief's nephew wants us to do this project, and he is helping us persuade the younger voting members of the tribe. We plan to present these materials at their next tribal meeting, this Saturday. We need to allay their fears. I think they see the disaster at our last construction project as a bad sign. It's making them hesitate. The chief is tough, and the people listen to him. We got started last year, but the survey team was lost on the reservation. We don't have a clue what happened to them.

"The chief, well, he looks squeaky clean. He's never been charged with any wrongdoing. There is no evidence against him, but he might have been behind it. No bodies were ever found. It's dangerous country. The current maps are incomplete of this very remote area. Satellite imaging is not of much use due to heavy vegetation, even in the winter. We're sending another survey team tomorrow to try again."

"Good," Andrew said. "You know how important this project is to us."

"Since it's remote, we'll build an airport," said Bob. "We will only cater to elite clients from around the world. The one percent of the one percent. With this clientele, we should see profits soon. We will build a beautiful resort for them."

"Yes, we will," replied Ron Barker, the third largest stockholder in the company.

"Can't we just pay this man off?" Jeff Rollins asked. His bank, Rainwood American, was heavily invested in Big Deal Construction Inc., and he had been a member of the board for twenty years.

"No. This chief doesn't care about money. He just wants his people and their ways not to change. We already tried that method of persuasion. He can't be bought."

"Andrew, you can be in charge of public relations with the younger people. Talk to them about the progress, change, and prosperity that we can create for them."

"I will not let our company down!" Andrew said. "No matter what."

"I move the meeting adjourn," Ron Barker said.

"I second," Jeff Rollins added.

"The meeting is adjourned until next week." Bob slammed the gavel down with a heavy blow.

Everyone left the meeting room, except Andrew. He walked up to a portrait of his father on the wall. Under his breath he said, "They'll never take this company from us, Dad. I will control it someday."

Then Andrew walked around the table and stood at the twenty-foot high, wall of tinted glass window that looked down on Memphis and over the Mississippi River. He began to organize his thoughts and plan his pitch to the Quan Pawtee people. He would appeal to the younger crowd and the women. Pictures of other villages that had been transformed by casino tax money should do the trick. New, modern homes for the women and fancy cars for the young families would be a strong sell. Photos of beautiful young women who would be visiting their area would appeal to the young men.

When he had organized his thoughts, he made a fist with his right hand and slammed it into the palm of his left. He knew, now, that his plan would work. Andrew smiled, pleased with his decision and his plans. He pulled the heavy chair out from the head of the table. He sat down, putting both of his hands straight in front of him so that his elbows could comfortably rest on the edge. Andrew imagined what it would be like for him to chair the board meeting. His hands moved back and forth across the desk in front of him, and then he felt the smooth leather on the chair arm, again.

The company was rightfully his. This chair belonged to him. He should sit at the head of the table. His uncle was old fashioned and traditional. Bob was tied down to old ways of administration and inefficient handling of the work staff. Many times Bob would keep workers on payroll that he did not need just because he knew the faithful, longtime employee had a family to support.

Bob had been mostly successful, but that success was nothing like it could have been, had he been more flexible and tough, to Andrew's way of thinking. *If I could just be successful in getting this Missouri deal to work and save the company, I could push Bob out.* He just knew that he could!

TREASURE MAP

TWO MEN STOOD TOGETHER LOOKING AT CHARTS OF the southeastern Missouri backwoods. They were on one of the most sacred parts of the Indian Reservation without permission. This area was what the company wanted surveyed and mapped.

Big Deal Inc. was known as a "can do" operation. They had completed numerous projects around the country, and while some people thought the company had links to organized crime, no proof had ever been found.

"We shouldn't be here," said Joe Knotter. "You know that old chief, Bear Daddy, gets crazy over this place. I heard that the last two-man crew, before us, was caught. Before they disappeared, they reported that the old chief stopped them with a double-barreled shotgun, which he pulled out from behind the seat of his old truck. Yep, they disappeared and nobody knows what happened to them. Everybody thinks it was the chief."

"That's not what happened at all, Joe," replied Jim Barstow. "I heard they were caught in a severe thunderstorm that created flash flooding and were lost in the rushing waters. A big search was made, but they were never found. This is a remote area, located in dense backwoods, with plenty of bear, big cats, and wolves. You know how their bodies could disappear. It had nothing to do with these people on the reservation. That survey group went into the wilderness at the wrong time of the year and they were not prepared."

Jim nodded his head in a knowing way and contemplated his thoughts. That is what he had been told by the top brass in the company, and it was good enough for him.

"Let's get this survey done and get out of here. This place gives me the creeps," Jim said.

"I'm with you on that one," Joe said and gave a mechanical smile. He picked up his transit, a surveying instrument, and moved it into position. "I'll walk it off, and you can catch me on the next ridge. I'll keep my two-way radio turned on."

"Watch out for the chief!" Jim laughed.

"Sure, sure." Joe shrugged his shoulders and made his way through the dense forest to the next ridge.

A few minutes later, Jim's radio cracked and came to life. The transmission was full of static, which was typical for this type of terrain.

"Jim, Jim! Something is not right! They're all around me! Everywhere! Come quick! Help!"

The radio went silent.

"Joe! Hold on, I'm on my way!"

Jim ran to their service truck, felt under the seat, and grabbed his nine-millimeter Smith and Wesson automatic pistol. He always felt safer having it there when he traveled. He checked the clip and put a round in the chamber. Jim made sure that the safety was on, stuck the pistol in his belt, and charged off as hard as he could run in the direction that Joe had gone earlier.

Jim felt his legs get heavy as he ran. He told himself that he would have to start exercising as soon as this job was done. Then over the radio he heard Joe yell again.

"NO! NO! Stop! Ahh!"

When Jim came to the top of the ridge, there in front of him on the trail, laid Joe. He was on his side with his back toward Jim. He was still holding his transit pole in his hand.

Jim looked all around and could see no one, but just in case he took the safety off his pistol.

"Joe! Joe! Are you all right?"

There was no movement, so Jim knelt down and started to pull him over onto his back so he could check for a pulse.

"Got ya!" Suddenly, Joe turned over on his own power, doubled up with laughter. "Wait till they hear about this one back at the office. Ha-ha. Scared you, huh?"

"This is the second time this month that you've pulled one of your practical jokes on me, Joe. Not funny. You idiot, I could have shot someone or had a heart attack. That's not funny."

Jim turned and walked back toward the base and his transit.

"Hey, Jim, I'm sorry. Don't take it so personal. I won't do it again, I promise."

"Sure, now get back to work before I use you for target practice."

Joe made a mock salute. "Yes, sir, commander. I won't cry wolf again."

Jim finally felt his heart stop pounding as he neared the truck. He unloaded the pistol, put it back under the seat, and took his binoculars and began to scan the hilltops. He picked up Joe on the second hill that he sighted, trained the transit on his location, and documented the spot on the master chart.

"Joe, I got a fix on your spot. Move on over to the next hilltop ridge," Jim said into the two-way radio.

"OK, Jim. Hey, no hard feelings?"

"No hard feelings," Jim replied reluctantly.

"We'll have time to finish if we can get to this next spot and back before dark," Joe said.

"Go for it."

"Out."

Joe left at full trot. He worked his way down the trail, not looking to either side. He had spent most of his life outdoors and was at home in the woods. Jim sat down and charted the area on his map and then stored the papers in a portable file box. He waited for Joe to contact him.

The sun was setting, and the valley had grown still when Jim's radio exploded into life.

"Jim! Jim! Come quick! Come quick!"

Static.

"Need help!"

Static again came over the small radio. The voice on the other end was Joe's, and it sounded like he was in trouble again. "No! Stop! Ahhh!"

Then silence.

"Joe! Joe! Come in. Over. Joe! Joe! Come on. It's too late for that trick. Don't cry wolf again!"

But the radio returned nothing but silence.

"I'm not falling for that act again, man! Grow up!"

Silence, again.

"Joe, come on now. Put your survey flag up. We need to get back."

Jim was getting mad now. He cursed under his breath as he went to get his pistol again. He loaded it again and stuck the revolver into his belt and ran down into the thick weeds in the direction that Joe took earlier.

"Joe, if this is another false alarm, I'm going to get another partner. Over," Jim said into the two-way radio. He held it to his ear just long enough to catch any reply.

Nothing.

Jim switched the radio off, hooked the device onto his belt, and jogged a little faster over the rough terrain. He got a little angrier the closer that he came to the place where he thought Joe would be.

Just up ahead, Jim saw him.

"Joe! Get up, Joe!" Jim yelled when he saw Joe lying face down on the ground. "I've had enough of your sick jokes! I'm not going to keep working with you if this is all you want to do. Get up!"

Jim kicked Joe lightly on the thigh. There was no response.

"This is too much." Jim pushed hard enough to roll Joe over. Then Jim saw a gaping wound across Joe's neck and realized that the leaves and pine needles were soaked in his blood.

"Oh, God!! No!"

Jim quickly felt for a pulse and found none. All of a sudden, the thought struck him that the attacker might still be close. Jim pulled his pistol and surveyed the area. Then the reality struck him. Joe had been murdered!

TRIBAL MEETING

"JOHN, THIS IS BEAR DADDY. I'M CALLING TO MAKE SURE you'll be at our Tribal Council meeting tomorrow. I need support, and an expert like you would give my arguments credibility."

"Sure, Bear Daddy. Look, do you think it would be OK to bring Mary? I haven't been able to spend much time with her lately."

"Sure, Conners, sure! I would love to see her as well. You know, John, women are not customarily a part of our council. But I have made an exception for tomorrow's meeting. Much of what the construction company is offering would affect the women. It would put me in a bad light to exclude them. I must be as open as possible to everyone. The women will also have a vote."

"I am honored that you will have her attend. Thanks, Bear Daddy," John said humbly.

"See you all there," replied Bear Daddy as he hung up his phone.

John immediately dialed his best girl's number.

"Mary? It's me. Chief Bear Daddy just called to verify my attendance at the tribal meeting, Saturday. You're invited, too. I mentioned this earlier, but I want to make sure you can go with me. I-I haven't gotten to see you much. I'll pack a picnic, and we'll sort of make it a real date, too."

"John, I'd love to go. Don't forget, OK?"

"Sure, I won't. See you at 4:00 a.m. It's a long drive."

"Good, John. See you tomorrow. This sounds exciting!"

John slept well that night and arose early the next morning.

Bear Daddy was not so fortunate. He had one nightmare after another. He was up before daylight, but not in high spirits. He readied himself for the day.

"Bear Daddy, I ironed your white shirt for you," his wife said. "You want to look your best when you speak at the meeting today. We have toast and scrambled eggs for breakfast."

"Marty, you always take such good care of me," replied Bear Daddy. "I don't know what I would do without you."

"I know this is important for you and for our people, but you must be fair and listen to both sides, Bear Daddy."

"You're right. It will be difficult, but we will hear and consider it all. My young relative leads the opposition, you know. The ones that follow him are all young and no longer respect our old ways."

Marty nodded in agreement, brushing crumbs of toast from her sleeve.

"It is easy to persuade them with the promise of opportunity and a lot of outside investment," Bear Daddy continued. "They don't understand what they are getting into. This company is offering a lot of fast, unproven ideas and easy money. You can't tell the younger generation anything. They don't even know how to hunt or fish anymore without electronic devices!"

"Bear Daddy, everything changes. Sometimes you need to compromise. Help them see what good it will do to understand your view, but realize that some change may be good, also."

"OK, OK. But don't expect me to just give up."

"I know you too well for that." Marty smiled.

John and Mary met Bear Daddy at the gate at ten that morning. They spent a few hours visiting with Bear Daddy and Marty in their home, and enjoying the view from their porch.

Later that day, the meeting hall was crowded. There was standing room only. Those without a chair would sit on the floor when the chief spoke. Every tribal member had an opinion and wanted to be heard.

The leaders of the tribe were all seated in chairs placed to either side of the podium. The construction company officials were ready to present their proposals and were seated off stage, in the left front corner of the hall. They would access the stage by a small portable metal stairway.

Bear Daddy sat quietly, center stage. His eyes combed the crowd. Before him was a locked ballot box. Slowly, he rose up from his chair and extended his arms to the heavens. Immediately, all were seated and absolute silence fell across the room. He prayed in his native tongue, in a soft voice. Only the elders fully understood the meaning of the chant.

One by one, each member of the council came up to the stage and spoke. Some were for construction and development, while some were strongly against it. After applause and cheers, it was apparent that about half of the people in attendance wanted development.

"Let us now hear from the construction people," Bear Daddy said.

Bob McGuire got up. In contrast to the casual attire of the members of the tribe, Bob, as usual, looked very business-like, dressed in a well-tailored suit. He smiled and addressed the crowd.

"I have a vision. What I see here is a new school for your children with the best gymnasium, an Olympic-sized pool, and computers for every child, and the best cafeteria money can buy. There in the distance is a parking lot full of your cars, owned by casino employees that will work in good-paying jobs inside comfortable and stylish gaming halls. When they go home, it will be to a new home in a modern subdivision.

"I look left and right, and there are upscale restaurants and climate-controlled malls. This will be the beginning of unprecedented opportunity for this reservation, and the members of this tribe will be the beneficiaries!"

A thunderous applause and loud yells went up from all the young people present.

Bear Daddy decided to allow this outburst to last thirty seconds. His eyes were filling with tears. He knew he must hide these emotions. Remembering Marty's words, he rose from his chair. Again, all were seated and quiet.

Bob McGuire smiled again at the crowd, then went back to his chair and sat down. He was very pleased with himself.

"Are there any more arguments to be made?" Bear Daddy asked.

Silence was the only response.

"I will, as leader of the tribe, make my feelings known. For generations and generations our people have lived on this land. Our people have defended these trees, lakes, and meadows. We have seen our reservation become the last pristine areas of forest and wildlife for miles around. If we give into these temptations now, where will it end? Will we lose our trails and ultimately lose our way? My people, make this vote from your heart. We are at a great crossroads from which we can never return."

The crowd was subdued. The older members of the tribe nodded their heads in agreement. The whole room was hushed, realizing that this vote was not as simple as it had first seemed.

Bear Daddy stood silently for several minutes, gazing across the tribe, his people. He broke the silence by saying, "Each person here will have one vote. Mark the ballot that was given to you when you entered the room, then place the ballot in this box. The votes will be counted in one hour. Thank you all for coming today." He then ceremoniously walked across the stage and descended the steps and made his way to the ballot box. He held his ballot up, as if asking for it to be blessed, and he cast the first vote of the day. Then he ceremoniously returned to his chair. Once he was seated, the noise level became very loud as the tribe discussed the issues in small groups around the room.

"What do you think they will do, John?" Mary asked.

"I don't know. Both sides have convincing arguments. Even if the Council votes for construction, the casino and other building can't be started without Bear Daddy's approval and signature. However, I found out the other day that the company does have a government contract to build a new highway through the reservation. They can build a reservation road one way or another."

At that moment, the county sheriff appeared at the back of the meeting hall with two deputies. He was looking and then pointing to Bear Daddy. A rumble of voices passed like a wave over the crowd as speculation was being shared throughout for the reason for their presence.

The sheriff walked up to Bear Daddy and said, "You're under arrest for the murder of Joe Knotter. You have the right . . . ." He continued until he had finished reading Bear Daddy his rights.

"Who is Joe Knotter?" Bear Daddy calmly asked, though concern etched his face.

"He was a surveyor for Big Deal Inc. He was murdered while trying to survey on the reservation. We got an anonymous tip that you did it."

"I've never hurt anyone in my life. You can't be serious."

"I'm afraid I am. You'll have to come with me."

The sheriff handcuffed Bear Daddy. With a deputy at either side, they escorted him to the waiting patrol car.

Nothing could have been worse for Bear Daddy's cause. The arrest seemed to weaken his argument with the tribe. When the votes were counted, fifty-five percent voted for construction, and forty-five percent, against. The measure passed, and Big Deal Inc. officials and sympathizers rejoiced.

"We'll start immediately," McGuire said. "Get them rolling. We know where the road needs to be. No matter what happens, the contract with the government is behind the construction. We'll use it as a springboard into the place. All we need to do is widen the old trail."

John and Mary followed the squad car to the sheriff's office. As soon as bail was set, John called Mark and they posted it for Bear Daddy.

"Thank you, my friends," Bear Daddy said. "I am innocent. They want to make me look bad to my people. Someone has set me up."

"I know, Bear Daddy. We've got to find out who has done this. But first we've got to get you back home. The construction company won the vote. They're going to start widening the entry road tomorrow. I think that the company will be turning it into a four-lane highway. With the government contract, I don't know how you can stop them. It won't take long to plow through the mountain pass to save time. I'm almost sure they will destroy the entrance to the cave and the artifacts inside. You know they use a lot of dynamite and big equipment. It will not take much shaking to fill the cave with rubble."

John, Mary, and the chief arrived at the chief's home. Bear Daddy got out of John's truck and walked slowly to the door.

"I will stop the construction people somehow," he said. He smiled and waved goodbye to the couple, his friends from Memphis, Tennessee..

"Somehow," Bear Daddy said to himself. "Somehow."

HAPPY TRAILS

"JOHN, THIS SITUATION WITH BEAR DADDY IS TERRIBLE," Mary said as they drove away from Bear Daddy's home. "Do you think that he killed that surveyor?"

"No, he's not that way. He's a good guy. There's no honor in murder. He's the kind of man that meets you, face to face, and looks you in the eye. He wouldn't skulk around and kill an unarmed man without warning. No, he's innocent," John said.

"I'm glad to hear that."

"Mary, would you like to see some of the sights this reservation has to offer?"

"Yes, John, I'd love to do that."

"I brought a quilt and a picnic lunch," John said and smiled. "It will be a little later than I had planned, but we can still make this a terrific day."

"Awesome, John. I love being with you."

"With all the excitement of the meeting and the arrest, I completely forgot about being hungry," John said.

"Me, too!" Mary agreed.

"And now I'm starved," John said.

The young couple drove up the winding mountain trail.

"It's beautiful, John. I can understand why the chief doesn't want it to be disturbed. Let's stop here. Under that huge sugar maple will be perfect. Oh, it's so lovely. I don't think I've ever seen the sky so blue and the leaves so brightly colored. They almost look like they are on fire!"

"The thermometer in my truck reads seventy-two. Feels good! I smoked some wild salmon last night and brought capers, fresh asparagus, cheese, and artisan bread. I also brought along a really good wine from Santa Ynez, California," John said. "I think it is the best."

"John, this is so thoughtful. You've never done anything like this before. This is so much fun!"

After a delightful meal, John asked, "Dessert?"

"John, you know I can't resist sweets. What do we have?"

"It's something I made just for you," John smiled. "Go ahead and open the last box in the picnic basket."

Mary looked down into the basket and saw a small rectangular candy box. She pulled it out and opened the top.

"Eeee! Oh, John!!" Mary gasped for breath. She blushed crimson. Her eyes had never been opened wider.

Inside the box of chocolates, between four individually wrapped candies, sat a stunning one-carat, square-cut diamond engagement ring, sparkling in the center. John quickly pulled himself up so he could kneel on one knee.

"Mary Morrow, will you marry me?" John asked in his smoothest, most sincere voice. He smiled at her with all the love in his heart.

"Yes, yes, yes! Oh, John! It's so beautiful!"

"Of course. But it's not as beautiful as you."

ALMOST-DOZED-OFF OR CHIEF JUSTICE

BEAR DADDY STOOD ON THE DUSTY ARKANSAS TRAIL IN the middle of the woods alone. He was waving an American flag, attached to a long pole. Below the flag flew the Marine Corp banner. Bear Daddy had served in the Marines during the Vietnam conflict and was awarded the Purple Heart for his acts of bravery in service. He felt very seriously about the flag and his right to hold his ground.

Unknown to him, twenty-five or so members of his tribe had silently assembled twenty yards behind him on the sides of the road. They weren't sure of what to do. They were still confused about what was best for their people. No one really wanted trouble. Everyone had had enough trouble in their lives and did not have the stomach for much more; but they loved their chief and wanted to honor his feelings.

Back up the road, in the other direction, a huge dust cloud boiled up behind three very large caterpillar dozers that were flanked by half a dozen dump trucks and other vehicles, carrying an army of supplies, equipment, and men. The logo on the truck doors read, "Big Deal Construction Inc."

The noise was deafening as they approached. Bear Daddy felt a presence and turned and saw his people. His heart almost burst. His eyes filled with tears, and he smiled, and then he motioned to his loyal tribe members to line up behind him. Bear Daddy turned to face the onslaught. The noise was so loud that no one on the road could hear each other say anything. They relied on hand signals and facial expressions to communicate.

The dozers were widening the road as they were moved forward. Several were fitted with blades that cut a tree at the base in one movement, while large hydraulic jaws on a skidder whisked the tree trunk away. Yet another machine would dredge out the trunk roots and fill and compact the hole with clay and gravel.

The scene ran chills down Bear Daddy's spine. He winced every time a tree was snapped from its roots.

The lead dozer reached Bear Daddy and stopped. The driver looked over at his supervisor.

At that same moment, a TV 7 camera crew from Little Rock, Arkansas, landed in a helicopter and emerged with satellite antennas and two television cameras, broadcasting the scene, live, across the nation. Soon a TV 5 helicopter from Memphis, Tennessee, hovered over the demonstration, and then landed with a news team. They, too, began a live broadcast of the standoff.

Bob McGuire was on site to oversee the work. Bob drove his truck into the area. He looked at the swarming news crews and knew he needed to take charge. He got out of his truck and shook hands with the road crew supervisor. Bob looked like a reincarnated John

Wayne. "I'll handle this situation," he told the crew supervisor, smiling with straight, white, gleaming teeth.

"OK, sir."

"I'll contact you later today. Get the crew back to camp. This is not good to broadcast all over the region."

"Yes, sir!" the supervisor said, and turned and waved to his men.

Bob McGuire walked up to the group of reporters and prepared to fight a public relations battle. The newscaster interviewed Bob and Bear Daddy separately. Afterward, Bob smiled and waved at the cameras, then walked up and stopped, facing Bear Daddy.

"Look, Chief, I don't want any trouble," Bob said. "We have a permit to pass down this road and widen and pave it, no matter whether the casino gets built or not. Your people signed an agreement with the federal government long ago giving the government the right to maintain this road into your territory. I have the government contract, and my company is simply improving this road. It's all legal."

"We don't want you here! Our people did not fully understand this agreement when they signed. I was in the hospital during the time the contract was settled and could not be part of the negotiation!" Bear Daddy shouted. "These trees are older than your age and my age added together. My father and his father walked under their shade and looked on their beauty. There is no good reason to take them down."

"Progress, Chief, progress. It's a new world. You need to step aside. Let your people move forward, reap the benefits of this commercial venture. I'll tell you what, I'll call off everyone today if you'll meet me tomorrow and talk this out without reporters and cameras around. What do you say? Tomorrow we'll set up camp here and talk it out."

"OK. Eight o'clock. Here," Bear Daddy said.

Bob pushed a big hand out and smiled. The chief stiffened.

"We will not shake hands until we settle our differences."

"All right, Chief. See you tomorrow." The two men turned and walked away.

Andrew could not believe what he was witnessing. A few disgruntled Native Americans stopped their huge construction armada.

Bear Daddy knew that he had only bought a little time, but at least he still had a chance to affect the outcome.

He turned to his people.

"Thank you for standing with me and standing for yourselves. I will call a special council meeting after I talk with Bob McGuire and make sure we all know and understand every detail of the contract that our people have agreed to sign. Even though people at our meeting voted in favor of the casino development, my signature must be on the agreement before it is legal. I do not think I can, in good conscience, sign those papers, but we will see. There will be no one acting in my absence this time."

The crowd of supporters broke up. The media left when they realized that all the activity had stopped and there would not be a big disturbance.

Andrew heard these words from the stubborn chief and was enraged.

Bear Daddy walked over to the huge, fallen oak trees. His hand brushed away the sawdust on the cut trunk to expose the base. He counted the rings. The trees had been growing since before the Spanish explorers started coming to the Americas. How many more virgin timbers would be lost?

"I cry out for you, my fallen brother. These people do not understand."

Bear Daddy spoke to the trees and to nature, for himself and for all of his tribe.

Bob started back to his truck and noticed that Andrew had walked away from the front of the convoy, looking very upset and angry.

"Come over here," Bob overheard Andrew call to one of the men who was standing in a group by some of the company equipment. The man in a hard hat started walking toward Andrew.

Bob recognized the man. He was one of a group of workers that had been hired at the last minute on the insistence of Andrew. The man had been a questionable hire at best. He was rough and unqualified.

The two men seemed to be arguing about something. The new man pointed up the road and then pulled a map and a compass out of his jacket. He marked a spot on the map for Andrew. Bob thought he could hear the man say the word, "cave."

Bob took a few quick steps to the side and hid behind a truck, directly on the other side, so he could hear every word that they were saying.

"You said I wouldn't have to do anything else. This is too risky. I never meant to get into all this. You did not pay me enough for that other job, anyway. The authorities would love to hear what you have done."

"I'll pay you double to do this!" Andrew shouted.

"No way, Bud. I'm not a murderer," the workman said. "When I planted that knife in the chief's toolbox, I believed you when you said that he did the killing of that surveyor and you just wanted to make the charges stick. But now I think maybe you did it. That old chief has a rock-solid alibi. You never told me how you got that knife, mister."

"Wait just a minute. You've got it all wrong," Andrew said. "When Jim Barstow found Joe stabbed, I was in the area looking over the reservation site. Jim called me to help. We tried to pick Joe up and get him to a doctor. I went back later and found the knife on the trail. In the excitement of the moment, I laid the knife down in my truck and forgot to tell anyone about it.

"It had a cloth around the handle, so there are no prints to be had. I didn't think to give it to the police at the time. Joe was not dead like we thought at first, just unconscious when we got him to the hospital. They couldn't save him because he had lost too much blood. A couple of days later, I realized that the chief must have killed him. He hates the company and us. Like I told you, that old chief is going to get away with murdering Joe if we don't help the case out. He was going to make our company go bankrupt. That's the only reason I want him out of the way."

"I don't care. It still sounds fishy to me. I think you did it! I'm not going to do this other thing. No, sir. No matter what you say. Let the law deal with him. Why kill him now? The old chief hasn't hurt anyone."

"Look, when I get control of this company, I'll make you project manager. OK? Bob won't be running things much longer."

"I said no, and I meant it. As for project manager, I'll have that anyway as a fee for keeping quiet. You hear that, boss?"

"I'll do it myself!" Andrew said and angrily kicked at a dirt clod. He glanced at the map, jumped on a company ATV, and sped off in a cloud of dust.

Bob let out a big sigh and slipped down onto the big truck's side-step. His head was spinning. Did he hear it right? He had no idea that his nephew felt this way. How did Andrew ever get so involved? Was he capable of murder? Bob decided to have Andrew followed by the company's private security.

GERTRUDE C. FORD CENTER WEEKEND

"MARK, PLEASE TAKE ME OUT. I'M TIRED OF THESE FOUR walls," Marissa complained.

"Okay, hun. Hey! Do you remember we bought season tickets to the performances at the Ford Center in Oxford? Here they are!" Mark said, reaching into his desk drawer. "Hmmm. Looks like we're going to see *The Sound of Music*!"

"Yes! Oh, Mark, that would be terrific!" Marissa said.

The drive from Memphis, Tennessee, to Oxford, Mississippi, was a pretty one. Highway 78 was four lanes wide, from Memphis to Holly Springs, Mississippi. The highway runs southeast, through the rolling hills of north Mississippi. Once they got to Holly Springs, the couple turned south on Highway 7. It was a two-lane, winding trail that ran down through the pinewood hills.

This trek bridged over small, spring-fed ponds, the beginnings of the Tallahatchie River that carried its water through the valleys that eventually formed Sardis Reservoir.

"This is such a beautiful day, Mark. The sky is clear and turquoise blue."

"Yes, I thought it might do you good to make this drive," Mark replied.

The drive took a little over an hour. Soon the couple turned onto University Avenue, then turned into the parking lot of The Ford Center, on the campus of the University of Mississippi.

The Ole Miss campus is one of the most beautiful university campuses in the world. Mature oak trees, surrounded by crepe myrtles and azaleas, are set against lush borders of monkey grass and endless rows of Mondo grass. Large beds of blooming annuals are replanted seasonally. Greek and Egyptian columns adorn the red brick buildings, each with large floor-to-ceiling windows, flanked by green shutters. Nature and architecture blend here to make a harmonious setting.

The Gertrude C. Ford Center on campus is a theater where presidential hopefuls have debated and aspiring actors have shown their best talents to an eager public. The center sits on the north side of University Avenue at the east gate of the university.

This Saturday afternoon, the Ford Center was offering a touring production of Rodgers and Hammerstein's *The Sound of Music*. Mark and Marissa loved to attend musicals and were especially excited about this production.

Mark parked their car, and the couple walked up to the ticket window.

"Hi, we have exciting news!" The Ford Center cashier said. "One of our patrons is graciously sponsoring a reception after the play, including a meet-and-greet with the actors in the East Room."

"That's really special!" Marissa said.

"Yes, that will be a real treat," Mark added.

They went in and found their seats. Mark had asked to have their reserved seats as close to the door as possible so Marissa could easily step out if she needed to get to the restroom quickly.

The house lights went down, and the play began.

Then suddenly Marissa cried out, "OHH! Oh! This is not happening! Oh! Oh!"

The pain flew across her abdomen again and again.

"Hold me, Mark. Help me stand. Get me out of the auditorium quick!"

The theater was dark, and the actors were engaged in their parts. Mark supported her and carefully guided Marissa to a padded bench in the lobby.

"Mark, I know it's early, but it feels like the baby's coming. This might be real. It may be coming this time. Get me out of here, please! Take me to the hospital here. I've heard that it's very good!"

"Sure, let me help you to the bench in the entryway."

Mark asked the docent to keep an eye on Marissa while he went to get their SUV. Marissa gasped for breath as she endured another sweeping wave of pain. With one hand, she held her bulging lower stomach, while she squeezed the bench with the other.

Mark returned and carried her to the reclined front seat of their Tahoe. He sped past the baseball stadium onto Highway 6. Two minutes later they turned into the receiving area for the Baptist Hospital emergency room.

The hospital staff quickly provided a wheelchair. Mark and Marissa were presented with paperwork to complete, while Marissa continued to cramp and suffer. While Mark filled out line after line of questions, Marissa's pain attacks began to subside.

"Mark, Mark!"

"What, hun?"

"I can't believe it. There's no more pain."

"What!" Mark exclaimed.

"I'm sorry, Mark. I'm sorry. I know what they are going to say. The pain seems so real. This is my third time to do this."

"Let's get you checked out anyway, Marissa."

Mark completed the paperwork, and the nurse came to roll Marissa back to an exam room. The emergency room physician questioned Marissa, and they both agreed that it was false labor.

"Mark, I'm so, so embarrassed. This is so difficult for me."

"It's OK, Marissa. It's OK. I'm just glad you and the baby are all right. We can see the play another time."

Mark leaned over and kissed Marissa on the forehead, which gave her a sense of relief. The couple drove back to Memphis and laughed about the many false alarms their new baby had engineered.

In an attempt to appear understanding, Mark turned his eyes from the highway and said, "Who could blame you? Besides, you're certainly big enough to deliver." As soon as the words left his mouth, he realized that he had made a terrible mistake. Big tears welled up in Marissa's beautiful blue eyes.

"I've hurt your feelings. I'm so sorry! I didn't mean it like that, honestly!"

"No, no. I know I'm huge. I feel awful, so ugly. This baby is kicking all over the place. I swear, I think I'm having a baby octopus! I know what I look like. I'm not blind! I just don't know what the baby looks like. Once I knew I was pregnant and all was normal with the baby, I didn't want any more sonograms. I wanted the gender to be a surprise for everybody, even us, just like our parents and grandparents for generations!"

Mark patted her gently with his right hand. He always had that loving touch that speaks so truly of deep devotion.

THE PERFECT DRESS

"HELLO, MOM."

"Hi, Mary. I hoped you would call today. How are you?"

"Fine, mom…. Mom, sit down. OK? Are you seated?"

"Yes Mary, I am. Why, what's the matter, dear?"

"I have something to tell you, Mom. I'm engaged!"

"Oh, how wonderful, dear. I'm so happy for you! I hope this lucky man's name is John Conners," guessed Kathy, Mary's mother.

"Yes, it's John Conners, Mom. He is so much fun and dedicated to his work. I love being with him. We want to be together always!"

"Yes, Mary, I really like John, too. And because you love him, I love him, too."

"Can you meet us Wednesday, in Barns Creek, Arkansas?" Mary asked her mother. "You know, that wedding dress place?"

"Sure."

"Great! I'll ask all my bridesmaids, and they can join us on that day. I'll have to call tomorrow and make an appointment for

Wednesday afternoon. I work that morning, but can get away by ten. That will give me plenty of time to get there. We can have lunch at Piggy's Barbeque Place, and then look for a dress after we visit and finish having lunch. Would that work for you?"

"Yes. We'll have so much fun!"

"Do you think Daddy would want to eat lunch with us, too?"

"Yes, but why don't you call him tonight when he gets home. He'd love to hear your voice."

Mary's mother hung up the phone. Mary's dad, Doug, came into the kitchen from outside and Kathy spoke apologetically. "I didn't know you were back home. I'm sorry. I would have handed the phone to you." Doug smiled, but tried to look puzzled.

"So, this is a big day," Mary's mother proceeded, finding it difficult to contain her excitement. "Mary called and said that John Conners has proposed. She is engaged to be married and wants to find her perfect wedding gown. She said she would call and tell you about it tonight."

"That is great! I have always liked John. Yes, of course, it's very special for our daughter. She has waited a long time and sounds like she's really excited."

"She is making an appointment for the dresses to be shown to her this Wednesday in Barns Creek, Arkansas. Her Aunt Polly will be there, too. And, of course she wants Elizabeth, John's younger sister, to be a bridesmaid, so she will join us. Elizabeth will be such a good sister-in-law. She also said she wanted to have her work-mate and friend, Tammie Doan, and John's friend's wife, Marissa. Do you remember the Bar-B-Q place on the highway where we used to stop in Barns Creek on our way to Little Rock to see your mother and dad?"

"Yes, though I haven't been there in a while. We always got great food every time we stopped there," reminisced Mary's dad.

"Well, Mary wants her bridesmaids, Aunt Polly, and you and me to eat there before shopping."

"I would love to eat with you girls. While you shop, I'll check out the sporting goods store. I had a feeling she'd call with the news. John asked me for my permission a couple of days ago," admitted Mary's dad with a grin. "I've always liked John and gave him my blessings."

Later that same day, Mary and Tammie Doan were talking about the wedding. "Mary, do you still want me to go with your family to help you look for a dress?"

"Yes, silly you. You're my best friend. Of course, I want you with me. We'll have a great time, Tammie. Elizabeth, Marissa, Aunt Polly, and Mom will be there."

"OK, but I don't know the first thing about weddings or wedding dresses."

"It doesn't matter. We'll have a blast! We will meet with my mother at Barns Creek. She'll have some great ideas. My dad is going to meet us there for lunch. In fact, that's my dad calling right now," she said as she answered her phone.

"Hey, Mary! I heard the good news, and I wanted to call to say I'm happy for you two and happy to get John as a son-in-law."

"Oh, thanks, Dad. That's so sweet of you to say."

"I thought I'd run this by you as soon as possible. You know I play golf every Sunday afternoon with my longtime friend, Sam. We grew up together. When I mentioned your engagement, he and his wife offered their property, which is a wedding venue called the Woodland Hills Ranch, free of charge. Of course, we would pay for the food, beverages, flowers, and musician's fees. The grounds include a beautiful chapel and a reception hall, cottages for out-of-town guests, and complete cooking facilities. You and John would need to select a date for your wedding when the place is available. They stay booked, so the dates of availability may be few. Would that be something you would like?"

Mary answered with a resounding, "Yes, Daddy! I have attended a wedding there, and I think it is so perfect! Give me their number. I want to confirm a date now!"

The office to the Ranch was closed on Sunday and Monday, but was open for business on Tuesday. Mary was thrilled to find an available date for their wedding at the Woodland Hills Ranch in DeSoto County, Mississippi. Although the date was only six weeks away, it was the date of her parents' wedding anniversary and things were falling into place so easily. Mary called John to ask if the date for the wedding suited him. He thought that date, a Saturday night, would be a great time for their wedding. Tammie Doan rejoiced with her. The rest of the day and night passed quickly for the two friends, thumbing through bridal magazines and shopping on the Internet. Finally, at eleven, Tammie said, "It's late and we have a big day ahead of us tomorrow. I'm going home." Mary laughed when she saw Tammie make a funny face, exaggerating her tiredness, and saw her to the door.

The two girls met the next day and drove to Barns Creek off Highway 40.

"That was a fun trip," Mary said as they pulled into the driveway of Piggy's BBQ place. Everyone arrived at the restaurant parking lot about the same time. They all entered the restaurant and were greeted by Kathy.

"Hello, girls," Mary's mom said.

Mary introduced everyone who had not met before, and the happy group gathered at a long table reserved for them and enjoyed a meal that was as delicious as expected.

After lunch, everyone thanked Mary's dad for picking up the tab. Mary kissed her dad and told him she'd call when they finished shopping. She then happily jumped into her car with Tammie. Marissa and Elizabeth followed them, and Kathy and Polly were in the third car of the bridal motorcade.

The Barns Creek bridal shop was known to nearly all females, far and wide, in the South. The owner of the shop was a smart business-woman who found and remodeled a turn of the century farm house, just outside of town near the super highway. The home offered an elegant place to sell all things necessary for a wedding, most especially, beautiful wedding dresses.

As the little caravan of three cars pulled into the hotel parking lot, the ladies gazed at the long row of picture windows. Displayed behind each frame of glass was a mannequin wearing a beautiful wedding dress. Each one was a designer gown. The choices were daunting, but very exciting for a bride-to-be. The six ladies exited the cars and made their way into the small lobby.

"I know you want to get started, so let's look for a wedding dress first and then we'll look for dresses for the bridesmaids," Kathy suggested.

After a rigorous fifteen minutes of filling out forms and listening to store policy, a sales lady sat with the group at a desk looking up different dress options on her laptop. The girls pored through scores of different dresses. They finally settled on ten basic styles to try. The shop assistant scurried off to pull the dresses and bring them to the mirror room where the dresses could be viewed and tried on.

"Mom, just look at all these dresses. They are all magnificent!"

"Oh, they are fabulous! Just remember, a dress without many sparkles and without a long train is best suited for the small chapel you plan to use."

"You're right. I really do want to stay away from too much glamour."

"I do want to show you everything," the saleslady said.

"I understand."

"Now, when is your wedding?" asked the sales woman, as she reviewed the questionnaire for an answer.

"In six weeks, on my parents' anniversary!" announced Mary proudly.

"Well, I'm afraid, dear, that most of these gowns require six months for delivery. But, if you can find something you like in this area," she gathered several dresses on a rack, "you can take it home with you today."

Today? That sounded great to Mary. Plus, these gowns had remarkable discounts. Thinking of her friends, Mary asked if the bridesmaids' dresses required the same waiting time.

"I'm afraid so," answered the sales woman, "but here are the sample bridesmaids' dresses in this room. Maybe they can shop while you and your mother and I find a dress for you."

From the corner of her eye, Mary noticed all her bridesmaids in a huddle. What were they thinking? What were they saying? Were they worried? Nervous? She decided to tend to the business at hand—her gown. Yet, things weren't as easy as she expected.

The bridesmaids and Polly wandered through rows of dress racks, touching fabric, occasionally pulling out a dress for a better view. "It looks like blush must be the color of the year," exclaimed Elizabeth. "Look how many blush-colored gowns are in this room!"

"I have a blush-colored maternity dress, but it only comes to here," Marissa said softly, as she indicated a length just below her calf.

"Well, would you mind wearing it to the wedding?" asked Tammie, not quite sure if she meant she could use it or didn't want to repeat something that was already in her wardrobe.

"Of course. I'd love to wear it, if that's what you and Mary would want. It would save us money on a dress I'll probably never wear again."

"Speaking of 'never wearing again,' I'd like to find a dress I could at least wear as a guest to another wedding," said Elizabeth.

Then Tammie came up with a great idea. "None of these sample gowns are identical, but I think it would look nice if we each selected a dress we like. The rules are that it must be blush in color and ballet length." Although the trend had become popular recently, Tammie didn't know she was on target with the latest trends. Every bridesmaid was excited and thrilled at the great idea and went about to find her own dress. Marissa, who already had her dress, found a comfortable chair and merrily offered advice when one of the women came looking for feedback.

Mary, meanwhile, found the perfect dress. It met the criteria she had always dreamed of. She tried on several gowns, but her heart led her to select the first one she tried. Her mother loved it, too. It was candlelight in color, perfect for a late autumn evening. She stood before a mirror, in the bridal gown, piling her hair up, imagining how a veil would fit around her head, when in rushed her friends.

Each was holding a beautiful gown, giddy with excitement to see Mary in her gown and veil.

"These bridesmaid dresses are really practical and pretty," exclaimed Mary, as the girls modeled their new gowns. It was decided that accessories could be purchased online. Within the hour, the mission was accomplished. All were thrilled!

"Now I want to find a place for the rehearsal dinner," said Kathy, as she placed the new purchases carefully in the car. "We'll need room for at least thirty-seven people. I know the groom and his family customarily host the rehearsal dinner, but John is so busy, that I think this is one thing we can do to help him."

"Well, I have a list of places in Memphis that I found in the phonebook and on a website," Mary said.

"Your cousin's suggestion may be the best choice. We'll check out the top ten places and talk to the managers and chefs. From that, we can select our favorite," added her mother.

"I want to eat there before we decide, so we can judge how good the food is on our own."

"Good idea," said Kathy.

"This sounds fun. Can't wait!" Mary said, fairly bursting with joy.

WEDDING BELLS WILL RING?

JOHN AND MARY WORKED VERY HARD TO PLAN THEIR
wedding. After much searching and sampling, they found a small
café in downtown Memphis that was suitable for the rehearsal
dinner. The venue for the ceremony and reception, the Woodland
Hills Ranch, was a gift from Mary's parents' good friends. It was a
small place for weddings and other celebrations and was within a
thirty-minute drive from downtown Memphis. The wedding was
planned, and now it was only two weeks away.

Marissa was due to deliver in three weeks, but planned to be
induced on Sunday, the day after the wedding. "It was so thoughtful of Marissa and Mark to schedule the birth of their baby around
our wedding," said John. Mary agreed and had thought of John and
his schedule and decided to tell him the arrangement she had made
for him.

"John, I know that you and your friends have made plans to search the cave this Friday before the wedding and that the trip has been planned for some time," Mary said.

"Yes, Mary, the chief and his people are really counting on us. We hope to find something that will put the cave and the reservation into a protected position with the government so the reservation can preserve the cave and the rest of the land. Jack really needs us to provide a more interesting storyline for him to report so the station owners won't be so mad at him for running our earthquake alert. They were really upset with us for causing a near panic in Memphis the last time we appeared on his show."

"Well, all of my family and friends agreed to help out by having the rehearsal and rehearsal dinner on Thursday so you and the others can go and do the cave diving and exploring that you had planned."

"Wow! Thanks, Mary! That will really help me out a lot. It was going to be so difficult for us to get back to Memphis in time for the rehearsal. I'll call everyone right now, and we can get everything set. I promise we will not be late."

John called Mark and Bear Daddy and confirmed the second exploration of the cave. He reminded them that they would all be using diving equipment and that they could start as early as they could get there Friday morning, week after next.

Two weeks later, John woke up early and remembered that this was Thursday, the day of his wedding rehearsal. The night before, he had packed his truck with all the diving gear and exploration equipment that he anticipated needing for exploring on Friday. He continued to make lists and pack last-minute items. Then he packed for his honeymoon, which would be a two-day getaway. The day went by quickly, and he turned his attention to the wedding rehearsal.

He took a quick shower and dressed. In no time, he was on his way to pick up Jack and Mark, who would serve as his groomsmen in the wedding.

John checked in with Mary by calling her. He let her know that he had picked up Jack and Mark and that they were on their way to the chapel. Mary said everyone else was there, and they were ready when the trio arrived.

The chapel at the Woodland Hills Ranch was erected in 1916 and had been used by a small group of Methodists until their congregation grew and they had to build a larger church in the 1950s. The winding entrance path and quiet lakeside setting was serene and gorgeous. Mary was excited to have such a wonderful setting for her wedding.

Everyone assembled at the church, and all the formal details were reviewed. In the background, the string quartet was rehearsing Vivaldi. The music sounded so sweet as the violinists skillfully pulled their bows across the strings.

The rehearsal went smoothly, and the wedding party had a great time at the rehearsal dinner. Mary kissed her groom goodbye as all of their friends and families bid the explorers farewell. Mark and John left for the reservation that night at eleven o'clock under a nearly full moon.

Each man took turns driving for three hours, while the other one slept. They arrived early Friday morning, eager and ready to get to work..

THE CAVE—HIDE AND SEEK

AT THE RESERVATION, THE EXPLORERS MET WITH BEAR Daddy and had a quick breakfast and talked over coffee.

"Bear Daddy, John told me that you took a scuba diving class at the University of Arkansas," Mark said.

"Yes, I wanted to see the sights under the clear water at Heber Springs and maybe search for ancient artifacts in the other clear waters around here." Bear Daddy grinned.

"You are always full of surprises, Bear Daddy," Mark exclaimed.

"You *are* an amazing fellow," John added with a quick smile of his own.

The three men checked and rechecked their diving gear.

"We're ready. Let's drive out to the cave and take a look," John said.

They broke camp and drove in their vehicles that they had previously left in the reservation entrance parking lot. When they arrived, they parked as close as they could to the cave entrance, so they did not have to carry heavy equipment any farther than necessary. Each man strapped on his heavy diving gear and carried duffle bags of supplies into the cave. Once inside, everything was placed on the water's edge in the cave pool.

The water in the cave pool was smooth and crystal clear most of the time. However, John did notice that light ripples broke the smooth surface in what appeared to be a steady pattern from time to time. He thought at first that it must be vibrations caused by his friends moving around, but several times he observed the surface break when no one was moving.

A twig snapped outside the entrance of the cave. Full Feather hoped that it had not been heard by anyone but him. Earlier, Full Feather had begged his grandfather to let him go to the cave and dive with the team, but Bear Daddy felt that the dive was too dangerous for his grandson and told him to stay home.

The excitement of discovering a new part of the cave was too much for Full Feather. In his mind, the cave belonged to him. He found it and he should be able to discover all its secrets. He stole away in the back of his grandfather's truck and hopped out as soon as the destination was reached. Later, he quietly slipped into the cave and peered around the corner as he watched the three explorers plunge into the cold waters, leaving only the safety lines to show their path.

Full Feather waited for a full ten minutes until he felt that his grandfather and the others would be far enough away for him to enter the water without being discovered. The old scuba tank that Full Feather strapped on his back was one that his grandfather had discarded years earlier. The mask and breathing apparatus were old, but Full Feather felt they would work. The air gauge read one-quarter full. Full Feather decided to swim underwater for ten minutes one way and turn around if he had not made an exit point by that time, so he would have enough air to get back to the cave opening.

Farther ahead, John and the others swam as quickly as possible. The water was cold. The only light came from their waterproof lanterns. In a few places the opening narrowed and the clear water was turned murky by their flippers stirring up the silt, which made their advancement difficult.

Soon they came to an exit point. The pool lost its roof, and a natural rock ramp allowed the explorers to come out of the pool on the other side of the cave's rock wall. They finally were able to take their masks off.

"Whew! What a break! It's not that far from the other side."

"No, it's just a few minutes," Mark replied.

"This water must not have always been here this way," Bear Daddy said. "It probably was diverted here from an underground stream to hide the second room of this cave from intruders."

"I think you're right. Your ancestors were able to walk here. They must have flooded this part of the cave or maybe an earthquake caused the water to fill this depression."

"Look, shine your light over there. Wow, it's huge! This cavern was so large it could hold a four-story building."

"Good grief, it's amazing!"

"Leave a lit flare here. It'll be quicker to get back to this spot. Tie off the safety cord and start it again right here."

"Let's check it out!" John exclaimed.

"Leave the gear here. We'll come back later for it. Just bring the lights and safety cord," Mark said. "Be sure and tie that cord tight."

The men walked on into the great expanse of the darkness. Lit only by the flare, shadows danced against the ancient walls and created a unique, surreal landscape.

Farther back, Full Feather got into the water and realized that it was really cold. His legs began to tighten as though they might cramp up at any minute. Once he had been under the water swimming a few minutes, he took a look at the old pressure gauge. The dial showed the air volume was less than an eighth of a tank. So close to zero!

He began to panic. Go back? Go on? How much longer did he have? How much farther could he swim? He peered into the darkness that seemed to swallow the beam of his light, giving up only a hint of what lay ahead. Could he get back in time? For a second he was motionless. There was no air now coming into his mask. He hit the gauge, but nothing happened. His body and mind were in a panic. Then he decided to pull hard on the line to let the others know he was here. He pulled, and to his surprise the line was tight! No longer freely feeding from its reel. Full Feather realized that it must be tied off, and at that moment Full Feather knew that he must be close to the end of the underwater tunnel.

He made his move. He frantically began pulling on the safety comeback cord and swimming as hard as he could, his lungs bursting, needing more air. He wanted to yell, to kick . . . anything to get free and breathe! He felt like he was blacking out!

At last, the darkness gave way to the light of the flare left at the water's edge by the others. This was fortunate, for Full Feather's diving lantern had dimmed so much it was almost useless. Finally, he broke into the heavenly chamber, full of light and, most importantly, air. He ripped his mask off and gasped for breath. His lungs were almost bursting. He choked and spit up water and gasped again and again. His coughing was muffled by the sound of a waterfall not far away. At last, his body calmed down and he lay on his back and gazed into the shadows, caused by the brightly burning flare that danced on the ceiling of the vast underground chamber.

Up ahead, in the second chamber, the explorers encountered a beautiful rock statue of a giant bear. In the same area of the chamber were bowls filled with gold, silver, and diamonds.

John flashed his light on the treasure.

"Wow! I can't believe it! I've never seen any treasure like this in any of the sites that we've ever uncovered anywhere in this area of the southern United States. There's no record of gold anywhere along the Mississippi River."

"It must have been left here a long time ago," Mark said. "Look over there! That looks like some writing on that stone. It looks a lot like one of those rune stones." He pointed his light toward the stone.

"Could be, but don't jump to any conclusions," warned John. "This could be something big, or it could be a hoax. One thing is certain, it is truly unique."

Bear Daddy said, "My people do speak of a yellow bear and sparkling rocks, the stars from heaven that rained down on our ancestors. I never really thought the legends were about something like this. I always thought they were just stories created to make a point, something imaginary, rather than real, physical objects. I never thought the legends were about this!"

Bear Daddy was awestruck.

Little known to the explorers, and even to Full Feather, Andrew McGuire had entered the cave two hours before anybody else. Andrew had arrived before the explorers, had hidden his truck, and then hid himself. Andrew had climbed onto the rocky ledge high on the cave wall, above and behind the main path and was quietly hiding in the shadows.

There was someone else in the cave, too. Bob was suspicious of Andrew's activity when he noticed scuba gear in Andrew's truck at work. It did not take long for Bob to decide to keep a watch out for his nephew. By Thursday at noon, Bob had rented a truck and loaded his own scuba gear and supplies and was right behind Andrew on the road to Missouri. After parking the rented vehicle some distance from the cave, Bob had to carry his equipment and hide in the woods, waiting to see what would happen. He was out of breath but determined to keep up with his nephew. He stayed outside the cave, hidden, and witnessed Andrew when he made his entrance into the cave. Andrew had been hiding in the cave for over an hour, when Bob heard a truck coming down the road. He knew it must be the explorers, so he, too, entered the cold waters of the cave and swam to an area above the surface of the water, then ascended to an indention in the wall. Both McGuire men were hidden in different parts of the cave just past the watery entrance. Andrew was unaware that Bob had entered the cave, as Bob was a very experienced diver and was quite stealthy.

They watched John, Mark, and Bear Daddy as they swam to the platform and set up their safety ropes. The explorers were all going in different directions and looking for any secrets the cave might hold. "I want to see if that is another chamber entrance up there," Bear Daddy said.

He began to climb up the steep cave wall right below Andrew. As in the other chamber, a giant crack in the floor was directly below them, wide-open, dark, and deep.

"Be careful, Bear Daddy!" John shouted. "That rock is wet and slippery."

"I will be. I just want to get a little higher."

Bear Daddy was almost directly below Andrew now. The explorers could see neither Andrew nor Andrew's uncle. The explorers busied themselves with photographing all the artifacts and looking at the many cave paintings.

Bear Daddy pulled his flashlight over the top of the ledge and ran the beam along the wall. Then his foot slipped, the flashlight came out of his hand and rolled along a shelf of rock that was below his waist. He felt the strain in his arm and searched around desperately with his free foot for support. The cave floor was a good thirty-five feet below, rocky and rough, and slanted immediately into the crevice. Bear Daddy's fingers and back ached. Little pieces of rock crumbled and hit him in the face and eyes, from above, as they fell.

Bear Daddy thought that the rock was unstable from all the recent earthquake activity. He never would have imagined that it was coming from Andrew up above, wedging himself between the cave wall and a large boulder that was dangerously close to falling. Andrew pushed with all his might. The boulder was barely balanced on the ledge in front of Andrew, and it was directly above Bear Daddy. This was the perfect place to cause an accident. The others could not see him, and without witnesses, he had a chance to be successful.

Andrew pushed again, but the stone was very heavy and had lots of small gravel between the rock and the ledge. Andrew finally put both feet on the back of the boulder and began to get his pushes into a rhythm. The stone started to move.

Suddenly, over the rumble of the waterfall, through the dark, Bob shouted. "Andrew, don't do it! This is no good!" Andrew was caught off guard and quickly turned in the direction of the voice.

Then Andrew's foot slipped.

"Ahhhhh!"

The stone broke free, and Andrew and the stone went spiraling down into the chasm, just missing Bear Daddy.

Seconds later, a loud crashing sound, paired with a death scream, burst out from the depths of the dark, rocky pit. Andrew lay dead, crushed by the boulder that he had dislodged. His uncle stood saddened and sickened that he didn't stop Andrew earlier. He never dreamed the nephew's plan was murder. He certainly never intended for the young man to be killed.

Bob McGuire looked at the walls and studied the ceiling. He ran his flashlight beam over the border of the wall and ceiling. He saw no opening that might go to another chamber.

"Bear Daddy, are you all right?" yelled the other explorers.

"Yes, I am," he replied. "Thanks to Bob."

"Bob? What's he doing here?"

"I followed my nephew here. He tried to kill you, Bear Daddy, just then. I guess he wanted to make your death look like an accident. I guess he was responsible for my surveyors' deaths, as well. I overheard a conversation between Andrew and a worker earlier and realized that he had some crazy idea that he was going to save our company by committing these crimes and getting the project approved. He would then take over the company. I didn't know. It tears me up. I'm so sorry. I guess he was trying to frame you, Bear Daddy. When that didn't work, he resorted to try to murder you. I swear I knew nothing about this. I don't do things like this. So I followed him here to see what he was up to."

All of a sudden, the floor of the cave began to shake. Rocks fell. Stalactites crashed from above. The explorers lost their balance. Their lights bobbed and flashed all over the walls. The cavern seemed alive, and great groans echoed throughout the space.

"The spirits are angry!" cried Bear Daddy. Then, as quickly as it began, there was silence. An eerie quiet enveloped them.

John's light had come to rest so that it illuminated a giant bear statue's head. There in an alcove stood a statue of a giant bear. Two large diamonds sparkled from the bear's face making the eyes look alive. Gold and silver treasure lay at the bear's feet.

"We've got to get out of here!" John yelled.

"You're right!" agreed Mark.

Another spasm hit, more intense than the first. Rocks slid down from the walls, and then Mark yelled.

"The flare at the pool's edge! It's out! It's out! Rocks must have covered it up!" Then another sound pierced the darkness.

"Help! Help!" The cry was faint, but unmistakably a boy's. Full Feather.

The men raced back to the pool's edge, struck another flare, and saw Full Feather covered with stone rubble, pinned to the floor. The pool was filled with boulders packed so tightly that no one could get out through the pool.

"Full Feather! Full Feather! Are you alright?" Bear Daddy yelled.

"Yes, Grandfather, but my leg's caught. It hurts!"

Soon the men surrounded him and began to lift the stones off his leg.

"Looks like it may be broken. We need to splint the leg. Once he's stable we need to get him to a doctor as soon as possible."

"Full Feather, how did you get here?"

"I'm sorry, Grandfather. I used your old scuba tank, but it's not working well. I'm sorry! I just wanted to be with you."

The quake struck again. More rock and dust stirred. The shaking continued. This time it lasted longer and the chasm in the floor of the cave grew even wider. More rubble completely filled the pool. The way back out was gone.

"Will we die, Grandfather?"

"I don't know, Full Feather."

"We'll be OK, Full Feather," John said and smiled.

"Sure, we will," Mark added. "Now let's get that leg splinted."

"I let the county sheriff know that we were here and to alert the Cavers Association if we didn't contact him in forty-eight hours," John said.

His buoyant attitude, meant to boost the boy's spirit, soon faded. "My wedding! I clean forgot! Forty-eight hours will be too long. We're supposed to be back tomorrow. Oh, no!"

"My wife's supposed to have the baby Sunday morning. They are going to induce labor. She's had so much trouble. I've got to be there with her!" Mark exclaimed.

The cave now lay quiet.

"Let's look around. We may not be trapped. It's possible that the pool was not our only way out. Bob, help us look. Bear Daddy, I know you want to take care of Full Feather," John said.

The three men retightened the safety comeback cord and dispensed it behind them to lead them back to the spot where Bear Daddy and Full Feather were. Each then took a flashlight and went to a different wall of the large chamber to search for an opening, leaving the boy and his grandfather behind.

Hours passed. Beams of lights flashed back and forth around the cave. Soon John and Mark returned and dropped down beside Bear Daddy.

"Nothing," exclaimed John. "Looks like there was another exit, but it's full of stone now."

"Same here," Mark said. "Every wall looks solid, and every passage we found led to a dead end. We do have emergency food. Let's eat and then try to get some sleep. We'll try again in the morning."

"Get Bob over here," Bear Daddy said. "He really did save my life. He didn't have to warn me."

The five ate energy bars and drank water that they purified with a small pressure filter.

Full Feather slept, but fitfully, for about ten minutes at a time. He would not get more than a total of thirty minutes of sleep, all night, at this rate. His leg was swollen and aching.

"Full Feather, breathe deeply and imagine you are far away on the mountain top. Feel the sun on your face and the breeze in your hair," Bear Daddy said. "Say your prayers, and you will feel better."

"Yes, Grandfather."

"Take this," Bear Daddy said as he pulled a little bag from around his neck. "Chew this willow tree bark and drink some water."

Soon Full Feather was asleep. All the explorers finally slept a little throughout the remainder of night.

THE CAVE—EARLY SATURDAY MORNING

THE CAVERS WOKE BY THEIR NATURAL BODY CLOCKS, having not slept very well. As they awoke, each one wondered how to get out of the cave.

Suddenly, an acorn hit Full Feather squarely on the forehead. Plunk! Again it happened. Plunk!

"Hey! Hey! Stop that!" he shouted, as he looked upward to find the source of the air attack.

There, on a high ledge, was a squirrel with one floppy ear who stood chattering at him. It looked like the same squirrel that Full Feather had followed when he first discovered the cave. How had the squirrel gotten into this chamber?

The squirrel chattered again, stood up on his hind legs, and curled his tail in an 's' shape, and then scurried up the side of the cave wall, stopping from time to time to turn and irritate the explorers with acorns and screeches. He went higher and higher, and then disappeared into a concealed crevice. Seconds later, he popped out again and chattered at them.

"Maybe he got in from outside that way. Let's follow him," John said.

The cavers rigged sticks and ropes so they could pull Full Feather up with them as they followed the squirrel trail high up the steep, rocky wall. After thirty minutes of struggle, they reached what appeared to be a shaft and ledge leading up. Soon they began to see roots from vegetation on the surface that had penetrated the rock above.

"Look!" Mark said. "It's daylight! It's daylight! I think it's big enough for all of us to get out."

"Come on! Come on!" John shouted.

The opening to the outside was small, but with a little hard digging, they made the space large enough for the cavers to squeeze through to the outside. The men pulled and tugged the ropes around Full Feather's stretcher to get him over the rocky wall, then squeezed him through the small opening to the outside.

HOMEWARD BOUND

ONCE OUT OF THE CAVE, THE MEN SAW THE TERRAIN had changed drastically. They saw uprooted trees. Large sections of land were broken apart and moved three to thirty feet, up and down.

"Marissa! I need to get to her now!" Mark exclaimed.

"Yes! Oh, Mary, I'm going to be late for our wedding!" John said. "We're lucky to be alive, but we need to get back to Memphis as quickly as possible. This must have been a major earthquake this time. Look at all these trees down!"

The cavers made their way toward their trucks and four-wheelers.

"I can't get any signal on my phone!" Mark said anxiously.

"Me, either!" John replied. "All the towers must be down. This must have been a massive quake!"

"Yes, you're right. We've got to get back to Memphis as quickly as possible!"

When the cavers returned to their vehicles, trees lay toppled everywhere. One tree lay across John's truck, but was small and had not done much damage. The group quickly picked up the tree and threw it to the side of the vehicle.

Bear Daddy's truck was completely untouched. Bob's Tahoe was totaled by a huge boulder. The men all helped Bear Daddy put Full Feather into the back of Bear Daddy's truck. John quickly pulled his truck back on the trail and Mark hopped in beside him. John drove up beside Bear Daddy's truck on the trail and shouted through the driver's window.

"Can you get Full Feather to the hospital?"

"Yes, John. Thank you, my friend."

Bob went over to Bear Daddy's truck.

"Bear Daddy, I know we've had our differences, but I never thought that you were a killer. It must have been my nephew all the time," Bob said. "He must have set everything up. I'm sorry. I'd like to make it up to you. Can I help you with Full Feather?"

"Yes, Bob, I would be grateful."

Bob quickly got into the back of the truck with Full Feather and waved goodbye to John and Mark, as he, Full Feather, and Bear Daddy sped away.

"Mark, help me watch the road for cracks and debris. There's no telling what we may find on this road on our way back," John said.

"I need to get to Marissa!" Mark repeated.

"Yes, I need to make it to my wedding! We don't have much time left. I hope everything's all right in Memphis. This quake looks really serious," John said again.

BABY MAYBE—SATURDAY MORNING

IT WAS SATURDAY MORNING IN MEMPHIS, AND MARISSA was off duty. She had seen the news this morning, and the newscaster had mentioned an earthquake in Arkansas and Missouri. With no call from Mark, she felt it must not have bothered the explorers. Many times before, the cavers had been underground and could not call out or receive calls. Marissa had begged them to have someone always stay outside the caves to keep family and friends alerted, but the explorers did not have anyone available for this exploration.

Marissa was cleaning the house today very early so she could attend Mary's wedding. She felt like a balloon filled with water. Waddling was a way of life. Picking up anything off the floor was a major undertaking. The baby bump was now a baby lump that dictated her way of life.

The bedsheets seemed unusually heavy today. This was the third load of clothes she had done after light grocery shopping in the morning. As she started to lift the clothesbasket, a sharp pain crossed her abdomen and continued to encompass her whole body. The pain dropped her to her knees.

Blood! Marissa struggled across the floor and made it to the phone and called the hospital.

"I need an ambulance, quick! This is Dr. McKenzie. Three Twenty-Seven Williams Street. Hurry!"

"Yes, we'll send one immediately, Doctor," the dispatcher replied.

Marissa hung up and then dialed Mark's cell phone. No answer. She knew that he was either out of range or still in the cave.

The team was supposed to get back from the cave exploration by ten this morning. *It's a long trip back,* she thought to herself. She pulled herself to her feet by pulling up on a chair, then leaned on the kitchen table. The pen and notepad was still there from making her grocery list earlier in the morning.

She quickly wrote Mark a note saying she had been rushed to the hospital and to get there as quickly as possible when he got back.

Marissa unlocked her front door, grabbed her purse and bag that she kept ready for delivery, and waited. The ambulance arrived ten minutes later, and she was quickly put on a stretcher and whisked away to Baptist East Hospital, Women's Pavilion.

Marissa was glad she had already packed her hospital bag and remembered to have the house locked up by the emergency personnel. The ride to the hospital was short and uneventful. Soon Marissa was admitted and taken directly to a room to be examined.

As Marissa leaned over to put her smart phone on the bedside table, her water broke.

"Wow! Looks like it won't be long before you're a mommy," her OB/GYN said.

"I can't wait. Oh! Oh! That hurts!"

"From your chart, I see some false labor in the past. This is within a day or two of the expected delivery date. Any more hemorrhage?"

"No. That hasn't happened again after the first time. It was just a little bit."

I don't think it was anything to worry about, she thought to herself.

"Good, I think you will be fine."

"Would you hand me my phone, please?"

"Sure, where's your husband?"

"He's in Missouri in a cave or on his way here. I'm going to text him again now."

"OK, we'll get you prepped. How close are the contractions?"

"Every five minutes."

"Was he in the area of the earthquake? I heard it was a 7.5. That may be why you can't reach him."

"Oh, no! That's a big one!" Marissa exclaimed. Marissa texted Mark and, again, there was no response. "You're probably right," she admitted to her doctor.

She sent a text to Mary next. Mary returned a text quickly.

"I am praying that you will be OK and deliver with no problems," the text read. "Hope our explorers only have a minor delay. I will let you know the minute that I hear from any of them. I'll miss you."

"Thanks! I feel another contraction coming. I am close now," Marissa texted back.

MID SATURDAY MORNING, DESOTO COUNTY, MISSISSIPPI

MARY'S WEDDING PREPARATIONS WERE IN FULL SWING at Woodland Hills Ranch. The wedding party had spent the night on the grounds in special little houses prepared just for the guests. A wholesome breakfast buffet was served in a large white tent under giant cypress trees. Mimosas and Bloody Marys were delivered with omelets, fresh fruit, and assorted muffins. The guests were happy and making light conservation. A misty fog lay across the lake, and swans swam lazily up and down the shallow water, chasing insects.

Mary walked from one guest to the next, smiling, chatting with each one for a short time. Her voice betrayed her calm appearance with its higher-than-normal pitch. Her hand movements were exaggerated, and her nervous laughter was uncontrollable from time to time, as the moments slipped away with no contact from John. She regretted that Marissa couldn't be with her on this special day.

Tammie Doan brought Mary an omelet. "I got you something, Mary," she said. "You need a few bites. Your mother asked me to be sure you eat something."

"Oh, Tammie, I can't. I'm so scared. Did I tell you that Marissa texted me that northeast Arkansas and southern Missouri had an earthquake late yesterday? Seven point five. I think that's serious."

"No, I haven't seen the news, but he'll be alright, Mary. He'll be here."

The hours passed, and Mary and the bridesmaids went to the dressing room to get prepared for their photographs. They fussed and fixed Mary's hair. Then they styled each other's hair, over and over again. Makeup bags lay open on the dressing tables. Empty Spanx cartons, along with instant-tan spray cans and hairspray cans filled the trash bins. The girls intentionally took their time primping to become more beautiful. As bridesmaids, the girls took seriously their role to keep the bride calm. They knew keeping hands busy would quell racing thoughts.

"It's time to dress you, Mary," Tammie Doan said.

The bridesmaids gathered around and carefully pulled the dress from its protective covering. The dress was a candlelight ball gown, fitted at the bodice with a full skirt and scoop neckline. The waistline was a Basque v shape. The sleeves were three-quarter length. The back was v shaped with a chapel train. The dress material was cotton batiste and had a very vintage look. They gently held it as the bride carefully stepped into the billowing layers of soft fabric. Almost ceremoniously, the bodice was brought up and her arms went into and through the openings. Tammie fastened a long row of tiny buttons down the back. The dress was beautiful, and Mary was beautiful wearing it. All agreed that it was perfect for her. The shoulder-length veil was secured to Mary's upswept hair. At that time, Kathy entered the dressing room. Mary's mother's eyes filled with tears as she witnessed the beauty of her only daughter standing by a window flooded with golden evening light.

Inside the chapel were padded bench pews. A simple cross hung on the wall above the altar and filled the vaulted ceiling space. In one corner, there was a place for a small group of musicians. The church was set with orchids, pink and lavender stock, Peruvian lilies, and lush greenery. Everything was very simple, but lovely.

The chapel was a wooden structure with a steeple and a green roof. All around the outside perimeter, three-foot-tall azaleas were in bloom. Junipers and nandinas were planted at each corner. Mondo grass lined the herringbone brick walkways. The building was on a rock foundation. The whole building glistened white in the late afternoon sun. A light mist of fog lay across the lake, giving the scene a magical appearance.

"Is he here yet?" Elizabeth asked.

"Not yet," Mary answered. "Not yet."

Then Elizabeth asked, "Did you see on Facebook that Marissa just gave birth to twins?"

"Twins?" Mary questioned in disbelief. "Oh, how wonderful! She is so sweet, not to mention brilliant. Tammie, may I use your phone?"

"Oh, Mary, you don't want to call John. It might bring bad luck."

"Yes, I do. I can't stand it! Give it here!! Now!!"

Mary dialed John's number.

"Please leave a message at the tone." The recorded instruction was all she heard.

Mary held the phone away from her at arm's length with both hands and stared at it.

"This is not happening!" Mary yelled at the phone. "Not again, John! You promised. Not again, John!! Not again!!"

Mary ended the call and went immediately into a fit of uncontrollable crying. All the girls gathered around, hugging her, patting her on the back, squeezing her hand, frantically dabbing her cheeks and eyes to save her makeup.

After a few minutes, Mary was able to stop sobbing and regain her composure.

"He was supposed to be here by now for the wedding photos. I don't know if I can stand waiting for him again. What has he done now? What now? I have given him chance, after chance. He disappoints me and then he's very sorry. But he usually has an excuse, and I know in my heart that he truly loves me more than anything else. I've got to believe in him. I just have to believe. He just couldn't help an earthquake."

She let the words go softly, as her facial expression left her looking lost. The light filtered through the tall cypress trees that lined the lake behind the church. She felt as if she were in a dream. Her bridesmaids' lips were moving, but she never heard a word.

Quietly, Mary walked alone over to the chapel and made her way to the altar. She knelt as she prayed in silence. When she opened her eyes, her parents were on either side of her, knelt in prayer.

OUT ON THE RIVER

THE MISSISSIPPI RIVER LOOKED THE WAY IT LOOKED A hundred years ago, moving slowly, only one to three miles per hour. The mighty river was winding, meandering, muddy, strong, and silent. Broadleaf, hardwood forests of oak, maple, and ash laid between the levee and its banks. Bald cypress and Tupelo Poplar trees populated the swamps around Memphis. The lower river was bordered with willow trees in abundance on the shallow outcrops of newly formed banks of deposited silt. The river had a history of constantly washing away and reforming. It had different features here and there, but overall, the scene that it presented was the same.

Today, the river was, as usual, filled with riverboat barge traffic. Some of the barges were going up the river, and some were going down.

Out on the river, just south of Memphis, the *Jim Dandy*, a huge mega-barge, plied the muddy water, toiling against the strong current on its way north to Saint Louis. This barge was carrying multiple tanks of liquid natural gas (LNG). The captain had made this trip hundreds of times before, during his forty-year career. On the water, up ahead, on the other side of the Memphis bridges, another set of barges slipped easily southward, on the complementary current. This set consisted of six units strapped together with huge cables and were loaded to the brim with giant steel beams.

Off in the distance, a flock of pigeons circled between the Memphis municipal zoo, to the Audubon Park, to the railcars of grain near the river, to the bridges that crossed the river. They would forage for food and rest on the bridge spans about the same time, every day.

Another riverboat, the *Big Easy*, was plying the muddy water, heading north, just below Memphis, on this Saturday morning. It was pushing five barges, loaded with freshly cut Southern pine lumber.

The riverboat captain had just refilled his coffee cup with steaming hot coffee. He sat down in his huge captain's chair in the pilot-house of his powerful river tug and, once again, looked over the approaching Memphis bridges. There were several bridges up ahead. One primarily carrying railroad traffic, one that carried traffic from Interstate 55 over the river, up to St. Louis, Missouri. The newest bridge was over forty years old. It carried traffic from Interstate 40, and its superstructure looked like the letter M and was lighted at night to emphasize the resemblance.

The Harahan Bridge and Frisco were the oldest bridges. The Harahan Bridge was constructed in an older method, cantilevered through trusses that carried two rail lines and a pedestrian pathway. The Union Pacific Railroad owned it. The Frisco Bridge was built the same way and was formerly called the Memphis Bridge. It primarily provided a crossing for trains run by the BNSF railroad system.

The bridge that carried auto traffic for Interstate 55 was known as the Memphis–Arkansas Bridge, or Old Bridge. The Hernando Desoto Bridge carried traffic coming from Interstate 40 going into West Memphis, Arkansas, on its way southwest to Little Rock, Arkansas, or north to Saint Louis.

The Hernando Desoto Bridge had been retrofitted to withstand a 7.7 earthquake. This work was done after the year 2000 at a cost of nearly $260 million. The Frisco had also had a $4.3 billion major renovation done. The bridge was over 125 years old, and the renovation was a great improvement.

The captain listened, as always, to the strong, constant hum of the two locomotive engines that forced his barges against the mighty Mississippi current. The barges were approaching the first railroad bridge, and the captain was aware of the importance of staying away from any part of the bridge supports. Gazing up to the sky, he noticed a flock of pigeons streaming on their way to light on the superstructure of the bridge. Suddenly, the birds began to fly erratically, zigzagging, reversing, diving, and fluttering out of control.

The captain set his cup down, and for a moment, he froze. Then he saw his front barges begin to lift out of the water before him, their load of timber thrown into the air like kitchen matchsticks, flipped out of their box.

The three-inch, steel-braided cables that held the first two sections of the barge strained and then snapped. The two crewmen at the front of the two-hundred-foot flotilla flipped into the air and landed in the water.

The captain stood to yell a command, but before he could open his mouth the whole ship, barges and all, lifted up so severely that water crashed over the sides and into the pilothouse, nearly capsizing the tug. The remaining barges plied on, and violently crashed into the bridge supports, bringing the bridge down into pieces in the water. A cargo train, approaching from Arkansas on the Harahan Bridge, careened into the murky muddy river below, falling with large sections of the bridge. The barge carrying the steel beams hit and ripped apart the underpinning of the Hernando-Desoto bridge on the western-most end and left I-40 with a thirty-foot section of missing highway.

To the east of the river, in Memphis, buildings began to sway. Bricks laid at the turn of the century gave up their hold on weak mortar and tumbled to the streets and sidewalks below. Pedestrians screamed out as the bricks rained down on them.

Streets buckled, heaved into the air, then sank fifteen or more feet in a fraction of a second. Water and gas mains ripped apart. In some areas, the gas ignited and exploded, leaving parts of the city burning.

Screams echoed from alleys and buildings. The violent shaking continued. The famous cable cars of downtown Memphis flipped over, flinging passengers out of the windows and onto the streets. Dust and smoke swirled through the streets. Sirens and alarms sounded to no avail.

Overpasses and bridges all over the city were torn violently apart. Power failures cascaded as the shaking returned, again and again. The sudden loss of power paralyzed city communication and caused a problem with directing emergency response teams. Traffic lights no longer worked. The cars and trucks that were on the road were held up in traffic jams caused by debris and buckled roadways.

The Mississippi River rolled and heaved, backing up at first, and then advancing like a giant striking tsunami. The people of Memphis had no clue that a thirty-foot wall of water, from a now redirected

Mississippi River, was on its way, pushing broken glass, shredded metal, and splinters of wood and other debris into everything in its path.

A 500-million-year-old weak spot in the earth's crust was in the area directly underground, below the city. It was a failed rift that had not split eons before as the crust formed. Over millions of years, the divide had filled with dirt and had waited until now to try again to rip apart.

Many places, not directly part of the New Madrid Fault, moved like the action of a huge machine causing the earth's crust to ripple like a wave, making its way across a pond.

"Just a seven to ten percent risk of an earthquake" was the daily prediction from the experts, but today was the big day. Church bells rang while no one pulled the ropes of the bells. Trees toppled and snapped. Sinkholes as big as football fields opened up all over the city and surrounding area. It was horrific. The soil was known to liquefy when subjected to heavy seismic activity.

At the same time in Arkansas, John and Mark had been making good time over the back roads. Most of the towns they passed through had experienced heavy damage from the earthquake on the previous day, but the buildings were one-story wooden structures that broke apart but didn't tumble down. Now the new quake started to hit all around the New Madrid area.

"Oh, no!" John exclaimed, as the road up ahead rose up and down like a wild roller-coaster ride in a theme park. "Hold on, Mark. It must be shock waves from another quake."

As quickly as it began, it was over. John had pulled over to the shoulder of the road. He and Mark decided to wait a few minutes to see if it were really over.

BACK IN THE MEMPHIS AREA

THE EARTH SUDDENLY MOVED AT WOODLAND HILLS Ranch. The little chapel shook on its foundation, and its single bell rang. Pealing away in the steeple, it rang against its will, furiously, with a lonesome, erratic urgency. It rang as if the dead were shaking it in frustration.

The small pond behind the church rippled, and the white swans swimming in the lake attempted to fly, even though they knew they couldn't.

The ducks on the pond made it airborne for a short time, flew in one direction, but then appeared confused and turned another direction. They did this time after time until they fell from the sky exhausted. The horses in the pasture at the bottom of the hill raced with their tails raised and ears laid back, nostrils flared. Because of the fallen trees and deep crevices, the horses' movements were confined to small circles, getting them nowhere. The ground violently shook again, with even more force, and seemingly, a longer duration.

Electric lines snapped. Transformers exploded. Trees swayed, and large limbs cracked away from the trunks and came crashing down. Everyone waiting in the church and on the grounds was caught off guard. Some were thrown to their knees, while others grabbed furniture to stay on their feet.

"Oh, God! Help us!" Mary screamed.

The sight was shocking. In other parts of Memphis, buildings toppled over, with fires blazing in some of them. Large sections of earth were several feet higher than they had been before. Roads were separated so far apart that they were impassable. On railroad tracks, trains were flipped over on their side.

As the crowd of guests assembled in front of the chapel, someone shouted, "Does anyone have a working smart phone?"

"I do," one of the musicians replied. He pulled the phone from his vest pocket and tapped the face, repeatedly. Then suddenly, the screen of the phone went blank. "It's not getting any bars all of a sudden. The towers must be down. Let's try a landline."

The result was the same. All regular communication was out.

The church at Woodland Hills was still standing. The foundation was conventional with a wide base. The walls of this one-story, wooden frame building were built with heavy reinforcement under the direction and careful attention of the builder. The plans called for metal straps to be incorporated at all the joints to help the building survive tornadoes, but it did equally well against earthquakes. The steeple had lost its backside sheathing, but the appearance from the front was unscathed.

Across the gravel path from the chapel, the reception hall sat with no real damage. It had been largely untouched by the quake. It was made with a complete metal and concrete slab foundation. The hall interior was about one hundred feet long and seventy-five feet wide. There was a freestanding fireplace at one end, built of wood with an aluminum inner lining. The building was constructed with thick metal beams and heavily reinforced concrete with a natural stone veneer. The structure all moved together during the shaking and stayed intact. The decorations were scattered, but only a few things were broken or unusable.

The bridesmaids scurried around picking up candles and straightening up disheveled flowers.

Mary had returned to the dressing room. She still held her bouquet of white roses in her hand. Most of the wedding guests stood in small groups outside, under a darkened sky, with their phones, trying to reach loved ones.

Then, there was a second rumble and crack. The shaking seemed to go on forever, although it only lasted less than three minutes longer than the previous tremor. Several quick screams were heard as trees broke and fell. Streetlights and utility poles crashed down outside. The electric lights flickered and went out. In the distance, more alarms and sirens joined the chorus.

Everyone was gripped with fear.

The church remained illuminated by all the candles.

"What do you want to do Mary?" the minister asked.

"I don't know," she said. "He'll be here. I know he will. I won't leave. Please stay! Just a little longer, please!!"

"OK, but only for an hour longer. My family will be worried. I've got to let them know I'm all right and see if they are OK, too," Reverend Holden said.

"Oh, John, where are you?" Mary said to herself. "I hope you're all right. I just know you are on your way."

Outside, a car pulled up in front of the church and the driver called to the others standing outside. "It's no use trying to leave. The roads have ten-foot-wide cracks across the lanes. They look like they are thirty feet deep. I've never seen anything like it!"

The wedding guests and staff close by ran up to hear the news.

"You might as well stay here. Two lakes have you trapped to the south and the east. The river has closed the roads to the west, and the cracks in the road and across the valley have closed off everything to the north."

"Surely the cell phone companies will get the towers fixed soon," Mary said. "I'll just text again, OK?"

"Let me do it," Tammie pleaded. "It will be better. OK?"

"OK."

Tammie deftly typed out, "This is Tammie. Mary wants to know if y'all are all right. Text as soon as you can."

"Mary, it says undelivered."

"Oh, no! My battery is getting low too! And we have no electricity!" Tammie said. She stared at the screen for what seemed like an eternity. She seemed to be battling something inside herself but trying to keep it a secret from the others around her. "I'll turn it off for now. He's probably out of range or maybe doesn't have his battery charged in his phone or the towers are all down."

"Oh, Tammie! Don't stop checking. I tried to get him not to go to that cave. He said they'd be back before noon. Maybe he's had a wreck and he's hurt. Oh, dear!"

BACK IN ARKANSAS

JOHN AND MARK HAD PULLED BACK ON THE ROAD AND cautiously pushed ahead. "That must have been a really big aftershock," John said.

"Are all the cell phone towers still down?"

"Yes. It was a much larger quake than back at the cave."

"I hope Memphis is OK. The girls."

"Just what I was thinking."

"We just have to push on."

"I hope we can cross the Cache River."

"Me, too." They traveled on as fast as they could.

When they got to the Cache River, the bridge had completely collapsed.

"What now?" Mark asked.

"I don't know," John said. He looked over the riverbank and then an idea struck him.

"See that big pontoon boat?"

"Yes."

"Let's drive the truck on the deck. We'll have to float across if the engine doesn't work. We'll come back later and take it back to the owners. There's no one at this landing now, anyway."

The two adventurers managed to drive the truck onto the pontoon boat, by using large wooden planks that they found next to a newly constructed dock. They were soon crossing the river under the power of the pontoon boat's ninety-horsepower Johnson engine.

They were on the other side in less than ten minutes and had the truck on the road.

After driving many detours, around fallen trees, overturned trucks, and large open cracks in the road, the two men arrived at the I-40 approach to the Mississippi bridge crossing into Memphis.

"Oh, no!" John exclaimed. "It's shot, and I think, so are all the other bridges."

"Man! There are barges turned over, half sunk tugboats. The city is on fire, smoke everywhere with buildings torn apart. It's a mess."

The sight was devastating. Large sections of the streets were piled with bricks. Multi-story buildings leaned on each other like a Lego toy city kicked apart by a frustrated child.

The Hernando DeSoto Bridge loomed in front of them, mangled and ripped apart on the west end by the gigantic forces of Mother Nature. Cables waved in the breeze. The large M section of the structure was still there but separated from both abutments, dangling and waiting to fall into the foaming, uneasy water below.

The two men noticed all the other bridges were in the same shape. None of them connected the Arkansas side to the Tennessee side.

Traffic was backed up for over half a mile. Trucks were abandoned, some toppled over, sprawled across the highway like a giant child's forgotten toys.

"What now?" John asked.

"Your guess is as good as mine," Mark replied.

There was a rumble in the distance.

"You hear that?" Mark exclaimed.

"Yeah, sounds like a chopper," John replied.

"Sure does. Maybe it's Jack and the Channel Five choppers. Have you still got that spray paint in the truck?"

"Yeah, I think so."

"Get it quick," Mark said.

Soon the men had put "SOS" in three-foot-high letters and "Help us Jack Mark and John" on the broad side of a turned-over eighteen-wheeler.

The chopper circled the bridge and came in their direction for a while, but then veered off when another section of the bridge fell into the water.

"Quick, John, get me the flare that you keep for road emergencies."

Soon Mark had activated the flare close to the truck message. The chopper then turned around and flew straight for them, then touched down right beside their truck.

Jack stuck his head out and waved the men into the chopper. Mark and John jumped up and down for joy. They ran, crouched, to the open door to talk to Jack.

"Jack, are we glad to see you!" yelled Mark.

"JJ, you never looked so good!" John screamed.

"Can you believe this?"

"I know the naysayers are going to be sorry."

"JJ, you know, we're supposed to be at my wedding and Mark's wife is due to deliver their baby any time. Could you get me to Woodland Hills Ranch and then take Mark to Williams Street?" John asked. "It's right off Poplar Avenue."

"Sure, I need to canvass both areas while doing a survey of the quake damage."

"Wonderful! Thanks!"

"Are there others who are injured who need a helicopter?" John was concerned for he had seen several accidents.

"There are forty-five choppers in the air, just for that purpose. We are not equipped. Besides, I have a specific job to make an eye-witness report. Get in if you're coming!" shouted Jack over the noisy helicopter engine.

John and Mark quickly boarded the Channel 5 helicopter and away they went, back across the Mississippi River. As they looked down, they could see that the river had divided into two major channels: one in the old riverbed, and the other coursing through the heart of the city, circling around to the south and returning to the original tract.

The broken city of Memphis was cloaked in clouds of smoke and dust. The Pyramid stood like a bizarre skeleton stripped of huge sections of its glass sheathing. The structure seemed waiting for one last aftershock to bring it completely down.

Most of the buildings in the old downtown area were built without steel framing before the turn of the century and had crumbled in the shaking. The parking garages turned into giant concrete and steel waffle irons. The structures collapsed, killing and injuring countless numbers of people.

Jack told the pilot to go southeast and look for the facilities at Woodland Hills.

The interstate normally carried thousands of cars and trucks from Mississippi to the bridge and over into Arkansas, but now the traffic was backed up for miles with vehicles trying to cross the median, crossing downed fences. Backing up and going the wrong way, just to free themselves from the traffic jam. Some cars crammed together, some wrecked during the quake, and some crashed into others as the traffic backed up. Injured people laid out on the curb and shoulders of the road with no hope of immediate care. There was simply no way to reach the victims. A report was relayed just a few moments earlier that floodwater had hit Baptist East Hospital and knocked out all their regular power. They were now using emergency generators. Water had backed up from the Wolfe River and covered the parking lot and first floor of the Baptist hospital five feet deep. The Channel Five station head C.E.O. instructed Jack to get pictures.

"We will go by Mark's house and pick up Marissa first," Jack said. "Then we'll all go to that Ranch and let John off and take you and Marissa to Baptist East, or wherever we can find a hospital open."

"Yeah, that's great!" Mark replied.

Fortunately, Mark's house was just off Poplar Avenue and had a large front yard. It was just perfect for a helicopter landing. As soon as the rails touched down, Mark hopped out. He didn't see much damage. The house was a well-built, one-story wooden frame construction and was thoroughly braced. The only damage he could see was the top third of the chimney in the back had fallen onto the backyard patio.

Mark quickly unlocked the door, noticed the alarm was on battery power, and he turned it off.

"Marissa!" he called. "Are you all right?"

At that moment, he froze. Something didn't feel right. Fear ripped at his stomach. A cold chill ran down his spine. As he walked on into the kitchen he saw the note that Marissa left on the table. At first he was elated as he read that she had already gone to the hospital, but feared she had had more trouble this time. He turned immediately, reset the alarm, and ran out of the house.

"Jack! Jack! You've got to get me to the hospital as soon as possible."

"What's wrong? Where's Marissa?"

"She's at the hospital. Something happened to her and she was taken by ambulance late this morning."

"We're three minutes from Woodland Hills Ranch. Let's let John off and then go directly to the hospital."

"OK."

"Oh, God, help us," Mark said. "I should have been there! I'm so, so sorry. I just didn't realize how important it was. I'm so sorry."

The Channel 5 helicopter lifted skyward, blowing leaves and broken limbs out of its way.

Soon the friends were landing at Woodland Hills Ranch.

John was the first person off the chopper.

"John! John!" Mary screamed as she ran to John, falling into his arms. "I knew you would come. I just knew it. I've been so worried. We were afraid that you might have been hurt."

"I almost was, but everything is fine. Sorry I'm late," John said, bringing Mary to him in an intense embrace.

The pilot turned off the engine. The people crowded around the craft. Jack, the cameraman, and the pilot got out and made pictures of the scene and quickly interviewed several people.

"Let's get a word from the wedding party," Jack said into the camera lens. He then lined the guests in front of the entrance doors to the chapel. In the foreground, he centered John and Mary, flanked by the bridesmaids on either side. Everyone was standing in place waiting for the photo to be taken.

John heard a familiar dog bark. "McTavish! " The little terrier came running up to John and excitedly jumped into his arms. John was equally as excited to see his dog.

" I thought it was only right to invite your roommate, so I stopped by your place and brought him to keep me company." Mary said, as she reached to give the little fellow a pat on the back. .

"These young people are here and are about to be married in spite of the chaos caused by the earthquake. Mary, John, tell us what this situation has been like."

"I never imagined that this day would turn out like this, but we are happy to be alive and we are going to have this ceremony!" exclaimed Mary.

"I'm the luckiest man alive. Nothing is going to stop us now," John added. "Let's get married!!"

"Yes!" Mary shouted and waved her bouquet in the air.

The crowd cheered and made a beeline for the church.

Mary stopped suddenly. "I've got to talk to Mark before we go into the chapel." She quickly turned to Mark. "We got a text from Marissa before the quake. Marissa is at the hospital, and you're a daddy! Twins!" she shouted, her face absolutely glowing.

"Wow! I've been worried sick," Mark said. "Oh, Glory, thank God. Thanks, Mary. Let's go, JJ!"

The camera swung back to Jack. "And that's how it is here. Love triumphs at Woodland Hills.. Our next broadcast will be from Baptist Memorial Hospital East."

Jack shouted to John. "We'll pick you all up on our way to do a flyover of Sardis reservoir. There has been a breach in the dam. We'll go pick up Marissa and the babies. Will not take long."

"Great, hurry!"

The Channel Five chopper with Jack and Mark left for the hospital, while the wedding party carried on with the long-awaited wedding.

"Jack, I really appreciate you taking me to the hospital," Mark said, sober and elated at the same time.

"I'm glad I can. The station will be happy if I do a piece on the situation there, too. I don't want to worry you, but the emergency generators are out at the hospital because the lower floors suffered flood damage. They are running on a small emergency generator for power now."

"Oh, no!"

"I think everything is all right, Mark, but we're going to land on the top of the building. You will want to get Marissa and the babies and take them on the chopper with us, if everyone is healthy enough to leave. As I told John, we will come back to the chapel after the wedding."

The trip to the hospital was quick. The chopper descended onto the rooftop of Baptist East. Jack and his cameraman got out to do a live TV spot.

Mark jumped out and opened the rooftop door. He ran down the emergency stairway to the first opened door he found, and went to the nurses' station.

"Hi, I'm Mark McKenzie. My wife Marissa McKenzie is here. Where is the birthing floor? My wife just had twins."

"The eightth floor, sir. You're not signed in. Let me see your driver's license or other form of identification." Mark quickly complied.

The nurse was satisfied and gave him a visitor's badge and told him the number to Marissa's room.

The lighting was dim since the hospital was running only the most needed equipment until the main back-up generators could be restarted. Mark was glad that Jack had handed him a flashlight as he left the chopper.

Mark hurried down the stairs and rushed onto the eighth floor.

"Hi, I'm Mark McKenzie looking for Marissa McKenzie in 808."

"Down near the end of the hall," the nurse at the nurses' station said with a smile.

"Thanks! Do you have a wheelchair?" Mark added.

"Yes, I'll get one for you."

The nurse quickly pulled a chair out from a storage closet and away Mark went. There was some light from windows and skylights, although it was still not easy to make out the numbers.

"Marissa!"

"Mark, is that you?"

"Yes! Yes, it's me," Mark said as he burst through the door.

"Oh, Mark! Mark, I am so, so glad you are here and you're all right."

Mark rushed to his wife's side.

"Look, your daddy is here," she said, looking down at the twins.

Mark was awestruck as Marissa pulled back the covers to show him two newborn babies nestled in their mother's arms. She held a baby on each side, one wrapped in a blue swaddling cloth and one wrapped in pink.

"They are beautiful, darling. Just beautiful."

Mark leaned over and kissed Marissa. He was overcome with a feeling that he had never felt before. He was so glad to be a father.

"Do you feel like moving?"

"Yes, I think so. Why?"

"Marissa, the hospital has flooded on the lower floors and the regular electric supply is down. The main generators are out, and the place is on small back-up emergency generators. The city has already had several aftershocks and no telling how many more are yet to come. I want to get you out of here. I've got a wheelchair. Jack is on the roof with the Channel Five helicopter. It will probably be our only chance to get to a good house for weeks."

"Wrap the babies up in their blankets and give them to me after I'm in the chair, Mark," Marissa said. "Roll us around to the service elevator. The emergency power is connected there, and it will take us to the roof. I can't manage the stairs. We'll have to risk taking the elevator."

Soon the little family was on the roof. Jack had finished filming two quick interviews with the hospital administrator and one of the key physicians. They had also done a complete 360-degree sweep of the flooding around the base of the structure and were ready to go.

"We're going to pick up John and Mary at Woodland Hills. They were just married. The city is a mess."

"Oh, I'm so glad that they were able to go on with the wedding," Marissa said.

"JJ has to survey the damage to the reservoirs in Mississippi for Channel Five, so he agreed t᷾ take us all to Oxford, to my parent's place at Woodbridge Estates. It's not far from one of the reservoirs. From the reports JJ has had, there was very little damage in Lafayette County from the quake."

The landing at Woodland Hills Ranch was quick, and the two couples and the two new babies were on their way again.

"Congratulations!" Greetings were exchanged as Mary and John boarded the chopper. Marissa pulled back the covers of her babies to reveal their sweet beauties. All were in awe of the two little miracles.

Marissa said, "I'm so happy. I have my husband, our two little babies, and we were able to attend our best friend's wedding, after all."

Friends waved joyfully as the helicopter ascended, not knowing what lay in store for them at home, or if they could ever get home.

DAMAGE REPORT

THE CHANNEL FIVE HELICOPTER SET A COURSE DUE southeast and flew as fast as it could for about sixty miles. Soon, a vast body of water lay before the reporters. The dam was over one hundred feet high and held back a body of water that was over fourteen miles long. Jack could hardly believe his eyes. The huge earth dam lay in ruin. The main levee was separated in its center more than halfway down, and water was pouring out at ever increasing speed. The water was a wild, seething, foaming torrent, impatient and unyielding. Jack instructed the pilot to fly over Batesville, Mississippi, which was the largest city in the path of the raging water, only about fifteen miles away.

Below, the small city of Batesville was in a state of panic. In the city, water gushed down streets and storm drains reversed and became fountains.

"Look!" Jack pointed out. "Oh, no! See that wall of water! It must be twenty-five feet tall! There is no way we can help them!"

Down below, people panicked, trying to get to higher ground. Some made it, but most just couldn't outrun the massive wall of water that crashed down around them. Whole families and communities were wiped out in an instant.

"We've just gotten a report from Grenada Lake that the levee broke there as well and at the Arkabutla reservoir below Memphis."

Jack turned to the friends and shouted.

"I'm going to set y'all down in Oxford and fly over the other reservoirs on my way back."

"Thanks, JJ," Mary said. "I don't know what we would do without you."

The two couples took a long moment to pray for the people in harm's way.

The GPS worked perfectly, and the group landed on the asphalt driveway almost at the doorstep of Mark's parents' Oxford condominium. Almost nothing had changed there, and it was a safe harbor for all the friends.

But in other places, much had changed. On a day of new life for Mark and Marissa's babies, there was much loss of life. It was the end, in so many ways for many, but for John and Mary, this day marked a new beginning. There was a deep sense of the value of life for all. For what we have this hour may not be with us in the next.

PICKING UP THE PIECES

IN THE DAYS THAT FOLLOWED THE MASSIVE EARTH-
quake, the city and surrounding areas were in tremendous disarray.

After the quake and aftershocks were basically over, the people that were left alive in the cities and towns, at first, foraged for
food, cooking supplies, medicine, and anything to make into shelter.
Those who were able to traveled by water or air to find another place
to live. Roving bands of gangs began to terrorize the neighborhoods.
Looting was rampant. People who couldn't protect themselves were
robbed, beaten, or sometimes murdered.

The National Guard Units of Tennessee, Arkansas, Mississippi,
Missouri, and Kentucky were called out to restore order in their
respective states. Once the National Guard and FEMA officials were
in place, order was basically restored.

Just pushing debris off the roads was necessary in the beginning.
When most of the main roads were passible, emergency vehicles
were able to penetrate to the areas that needed help.

People that had not been affected by the quake were organized by religious or civic groups and began to respond as volunteers. Churches made massive contributions of food, supplies, and manpower.

Tent communities and mobile home cities were quickly erected, and a general census was conducted.

One of the main priorities was the repair of cell towers so everyone could contact each other and relief could be coordinated. Loved ones could reconnect.

Barges were tethered together and covered with steel beams to temporarily restore emergency traffic across the Mississippi River. Some boats that survived the quake were used as ferries. The railroad companies donated the use of their spare diesel electric locomotives to provide electric power for emergency care facilities.

The Mississippi levee system was broken down in several spots, and the Army Corp of Engineers worked day and night to seal its borders before spring flooding set in.

It took FedEx two weeks to get back in operation. The pace was much slower, and the capacity was limited for weeks later.

The latest news reports estimated the financial loss to be close to $300 billion. 715,000 buildings were damaged. 2.6 million people were without electricity for weeks. There were 86,000 casualties and 3,500 fatalities.

People could only help each other as much as possible and say their prayers.

Later that year, Mark and John made several appearances on Jack's Channel Five, six o'clock news show, where Jack extolled the virtues of being prepared. At the closing of each news broadcast since the quake, Jack would always close by saying, "It's OK to cry wolf!"

BEAR DADDY'S PRAYER

BEAR DADDY LOOKED UP INTO THE HEAVENS WITH HIS hands held high and widely apart. He began to pray.

"Great Father I pray to you, please hear me and grant me peace.
Don't let me die alone.
Don't let me be forgotten.
Don't let me be unloved.

Give my life purpose.
Give my life forgiveness and redemption.
Give my life beauty and meaning.

Help me be the man you would have me be.
Help me make wise decisions for my people.
Help me keep the future alive for my children and theirs."

Bear Daddy paused, swallowed, and took a deep breath. It was a lot to ask, but somehow he knew that his prayers would be answered.

Special thanks to my wife Mary Catherine, without her help and encouragement this story would not have been finished.

Thanks to John Connaway, a real archeologist, whose advise and instruction have been most valuable.